THEY CAME TO WICHITA

Layne Britton—He hoped to quiet his killing ways, but once more his guns must explode into action.

Connie Lee—The pain she still bore from her unhappy childhood would lead her to greater dangers as an adult.

Dolph Catron—A cruel wolf of a man, ready to tear down any man or woman who tries to stop his hunt for greater wealth.

Cole Clinger—Ready to break his outlaw friend out of the Fort Dodge prison, he would use all the stage passengers as his deadly pawns.

The Stagecoach Series
Ask your bookseller for the books you have missed

STAGECOACH STATION 15:

WICHITA

Hank Mitchum

 Created by the producers of
Wagons West, White Indian,
and Saga of the Southwest.

Chairman of the Board: Lyle Kenyon Engel

BANTAM BOOKS
TORONTO • NEW YORK • LONDON • SYDNEY • AUCKLAND

STAGECOACH STATION 15: WICHITA

*A Bantam Book / published by arrangement with
Book Creations, Inc.*

Bantam edition / December 1984

*Produced by Book Creations, Inc.
Chairman of the Board: Lyle Kenyon Engel*

ISBN 0-553-24544-9

Published simultaneously in the United States and Canada

*Bantam Books are published by Bantam Books, Inc. Its trademark,
consisting of the words "Bantam Books" and the portrayal of a
rooster, is Registered in U.S. Patent and Trademark Office and in
other countries. Marca Registrada. Bantam Books, Inc., 666 Fifth
Avenue, New York, New York 10103.*

PRINTED IN THE UNITED STATES OF AMERICA

H   0 9 8 7 6 5 4 3 2 1

STAGECOACH STATION 15:

WICHITA

WICHITA, KANSAS 1872

Chapter One

A broad-winged hawk wheeled proudly in the blue Kansas sky. It circled several times, dropping lower, then swooped closely over the heads of the two men sitting in the box on the rumbling stagecoach.

Ozzie Gisler, driver of the bright red Wells Fargo stagecoach, ignored the bird and prodded his horses by cracking his twelve-foot rawhide lash sharply above their heads and yelling out, "Hee-yah!"

Shotgun rider Bill Henderson adjusted his hat as if the hawk had touched it. "If he comes any closer, I'll be able to pluck his feathers," he said.

Ozzie gave an infectious laugh and said, "He's just lookin' for somethin' to eat, Bill! Probably knows about those oversized bugs in your hair!"

Seconds later, the hawk snatched a wiggling prairie dog in its talons, then swooped in front of the coach and took off skyward. Ozzie chuckled, pointing at the prairie dog, and said, "See there! He got one of your bugs, and you didn't even know it!"

Bill cuffed the older man playfully, then took in the panoramic view, carefully scrutinizing the broad, rolling prairie for signs of danger. The September sun was arching downward from its apex. They would be in Wichita by four o'clock. Young Bill, who was tall and muscular, with dark curly hair and brown eyes, was anxious to get home. His vacation started tomorrow, and he was looking for-

1

ward to a whole week without riding a stagecoach. He loved working with Ozzie, of course, but Bill could stand to miss the old driver for a few days if it would give him a chance to get the dust out of his mouth.

Swaying with the movement of the Concord as it rocked on its leather thoroughbraces, Bill Henderson looked at Ozzie Gisler from the corner of his eye. A man in his late fifties, Ozzie seemed to have crawled out of his crib and taken a set of reins in his hands. He had jockeyed wagons, buckboards, buggies, and surreys all his life, and now the smell of horseflesh permeated his own hide. For the past five years, Ozzie had driven coaches for Wells Fargo, and just two years ago the company had given him his own run between Wichita and Dodge City.

Bill Henderson had been the driver's shotgunner since the first run to Dodge, and they had become close friends. Twenty-two-year-old Bill had learned a lot from Ozzie. He had watched with pleasure as the horses responded with precision to the man's skilled fingers on the reins. One day Bill would have his own coach to command. He would be ready, too—he had the best teacher in the West.

With affection, Bill eyed Ozzie again. He was long, lanky, and silver haired. His eyes had a permanent squint from too much sun, and his face, leathered from heat and wind, was the color of mottled brick. Always ready to tease and poke fun, the aging driver wore a battered hat with the brim flipped straight up in the front. Bill thought how lucky he was to be working with Ozzie Gisler, who was loved by just about everybody in Wichita for his warmth and his homespun philosophy.

It had been a hot, dusty three days from Dodge City. Bill reached down in the bottom of the front boot to get the canvas water bag. Ozzie's little dog, Puddles, lay next to the bag, as if she were trying to soak some of its moisture into her skin. Hoisting the twelve-pound ball of iron-gray fur up onto the seat, Bill said, "Pardon me, Puddles, but I've got to have a swig of this wet stuff."

Bill took a long pull from the bag and was about to cork it when the dog looked at him with thirsty eyes. Smiling, the shotgunner put her in his lap and made a trough of his hand. Puddles lapped water as Bill dribbled it into his palm.

Ozzie chuckled. "You talk about me spoilin' that mutt. You're worse than I am."

Bill put Puddles back on the floor of the boot and let his eyes roam the surrounding plains again.

"Looks peaceful enough," commented Ozzie.

"Just as well," breathed Bill, stretching his arms and tapping the barrel of the shotgun that rode next to his leg. "We haven't got anything to give robbers today. That is, unless they would want Puddles."

Ozzie said thinly, "Over my rigor mortis."

Changing the subject, the shotgunner said, "Too bad you won't be in town for the weekend. You could take Nelda to the barn dance. You know she's sweet on you."

The driver shook his head. "No thanks. If that woman got me dancin', she'd dance me right over to the church and down the aisle to the altar!"

"Now, Ozzie," laughed Bill, "Nelda's a right pretty woman. It's time you were settling down. I think if you married Nelda, she'd take some of the crotchety out of you. Besides, you need some female companionship."

Reaching down and lifting the little gray dog onto his lap, Gisler said, "I've got all the she-male companionship I need right here, don't I, Puddles?" Eyeing his partner with a squint, he added, "Fellow that's been a bachelor long as I have could never get used to a bit in his mouth, nohow."

Bill sighed. "Well, I'm taking Betty Ann Stewart to the dance. Don't you think she's one of Wichita's prettiest?"

"She's a cutie, I'll admit," said the driver. "But I want to know somethin'."

"What's that?"

"How come you never took the prize of Wichita dancin'?"

"You mean Connie Lee." It was a statement, not a question.

"I sure do."

"She's been out of touch ever since her mother got sick," said Bill. "Just about every young man in Wichita has beat a path to her door. But Connie won't hardly leave her mother's bedside.''

"I know she's mighty devoted to Cora," admitted Ozzie, "but it seems to me if a fellow wanted to take her out bad enough, he'd find a way to get her out of the house long enough for a barn dance or a stroll down by the river.''

"I don't think there'll be any courting Connie Lee until her mother is gone," Bill said quietly.

"Well, some smart fellow sure ought to be campin' on her doorstep. That little hunk of femininity is the prettiest thing to tempt a man's masculinity since Alexander fell in love with Cleopatra!''

"It wasn't Alexander. It was Mark Antony.''

Ozzie snapped his fingers. "Oh, yeah! I guess I just need to read my Bible more!''

The Concord was pulling up a steep draw. Ozzie Gisler put the reins in both hands as they neared the crest, which topped out in a narrow passage. Suddenly an old hay wagon rolled backward across the road and lodged in the pass, blocking their way.

Ozzie pulled on the reins, and Bill reached for his shotgun.

"Leave that shotgun where it is!" a stern voice bellowed.

Bill's hand froze as he saw the glitter of gunmetal. A wiry, narrow-shouldered man eased his horse around the edge of the draw as six other riders appeared on the steep banks, guns leveled. There was hushed discussion inside the coach as the leader of the gang squeezed his horse past the old hay wagon and approached.

Bill Henderson took a good look at the leader. The man was young, probably around twenty-two. He wore a black flat-crowned hat with a neck cord that dangled under his long, pointed chin. His entire outfit was black— shirt, trousers, boots, bandanna.

The stone-faced youth had straw-colored hair and fuzz on his upper lip. His black vest was lined with silver studs, as were his black gunbelt and holster. Even the horse he rode was solid black. Bridle and saddle matched the color of the horse and were also lined with silver studs.

Ozzie hollered toward his passengers, "You folks stay inside!" Bringing his gaze down to the yellow-haired leader, he said, "Mister, I hate to disappoint you, but we got no gold, no silver, and no cash money on this run. Honest."

"We believe you, Pop," said the leader levelly. "We're not after money. We want one of your passengers."

"One of my passengers? What for? Who do you want?"

Holding the driver with a hard stare, the stolid-featured leader said, "Layne Britton."

Ozzie's eyes widened as his head moved back and forth. "We ain't got Layne Britton on this stage, mister. We have a Mr. Adam Britton. But the famous gunfighter, no."

The six riders drew in closer as the narrow-shouldered man on the black horse said, "Now, Pop, you and your shotgunner climb down. Let me see your hands all the way." As Bill and Ozzie reluctantly did as they were ordered, the man turned to those inside the coach and barked, "Everybody in there come out and join the party!"

The coach door swung open. Two older men and their frightened wives were the first to emerge, followed by a middle-aged woman. The last to appear was a tall man, standing six feet five inches in his expensive black boots. In his mid-twenties, he had coal-black hair and a neatly trimmed mustache to match. Beneath his light-gray Stetson was a ruggedly handsome face and gray eyes, and his broad-shouldered, muscular frame was clothed in a western-cut gray suit with thin black piping on the coat. His vest was adorned with a gold watch chain, and he wore a white shirt with a black string tie.

The man on the black horse waited until his friends had dismounted and stood holding their guns on the group that gathered beside the bright red coach. Then, with a pompous flair, he holstered his gun, swung his right leg over the pommel, and dropped to the ground.

Swaggering toward the tall passenger, the young gunman stopped and stood spread-legged about ten feet away. "Well, Britton," he said with insolence in his pale blue eyes, "at last we come face to face."

Ozzie Gisler spoke up. "You got it all wrong, mister. This gentleman's name is *Adam* Britton."

"Shut your trap, Pop," hissed the man in black, eyes riveted on the tall passenger. "He's Layne Britton all right. I've been waiting a long time for this." A cold grin formed on his slender face. "I'm Pete Foss."

Layne Britton's face was like granite. "So?"

Eyes widening, Pete Foss said, "You've heard of me."

"Can't say as I have," Layne said in a low, even voice.

Foss's mouth fell open. Narrowing his eyes, he snapped, "You're lying, mister! You've heard of me, all right."

"Hate to bruise your ego, sonny," retorted Layne, temper rising, "but your name means nothing to me."

Pete Foss wiped his hand across his mouth and tilted the flat-crowned hat to the back of his head. Pulling his lip upward in a sneer, he said, "I backed down Sam Farley last week in El Dorado."

"Never heard of him," said the tall man, his patience wearing thin.

"I'll have you know I outdrew Francis Dix last month up in Newton. You notice I'm here to tell the story."

Layne Britton was weary of greenhorn gunslicks, and he could feel the hair bristling on the back of his neck. "*Frances* Dix?" he said bitingly. "I never heard of *her*, either."

Foss's face reddened. "Okay, Britton. I'm calling you." With that, he backed up, giving Layne room to move and put the bystanders out of the line of fire.

Levelly, Layne said, "I know you want to make a big name for yourself by killing me in front of these people, Pete, but it won't go over so good on the circuit when they hear you shot me when I was unarmed." As he spoke, Layne slowly spread his coat, revealing that no gunbelt hung on his narrow waist.

Ozzie Gisler's eyes were wide. "Jeez," he exclaimed. "You really *are* Layne Britton!"

The passengers eyed each other, shaking their heads. Bill Henderson, who stood next to Ozzie, spoke up and said, "You'd better be glad Mr. Britton is not wearing his gun. Nobody west of the Missouri can outdraw him!"

"You shut up!" growled Foss, throwing Bill an icy stare. He swung his gaze back to Layne Britton. "I'll give you thirty seconds to get the gun out of your gear."

"I don't have a gun," Layne said blandly. "I'm not a gunfighter anymore. You'll have to find somebody else to kill you."

Pete Foss bared his teeth, twisting his long, craggy face. Holding his burning eyes on Layne Britton, he called behind him, "Boone! Come here!"

A skinny young man who strongly resembled the man in black strode forward, gun in hand.

"This is my kid brother, Britton," said Foss. "You can use his gun."

"I'm through slapping leather," said Layne. "There'll be no gunfight here today."

"You're a yellow dog!" lashed Foss, eyes wild.

From up in the box, Puddles, who seemed to recognize these words, began to bark at Pete Foss.

"Shut that animal up!" Foss shouted.

Instantly, Ozzie stepped up on a spoke of the wheel and quieted his dog.

Holding his defiant glare on Layne Britton, Foss said, "You're afraid of me, ain't you? Well, I guess your day had to come, Britton. Sooner or later every gunslick meets his match. He has to either grovel and crawl away on his belly or die on his back with a bullet in his gut."

Bill Henderson ejected a humorless laugh. "You're talking through your hat, Foss. The likes of you sure is no match for Layne Britton."

Suddenly Pete Foss swung his gun on Bill and fired. The women screamed as Bill went down. Ozzie dropped to his friend's side, examining the wound in his shoulder. "Lay still," he said. "It's only a flesh wound."

Layne Britton fought to control his temper. He looked

down at the shotgunner and saw that he had been hit on the corner of the left shoulder. Looking back at Pete Foss, he said, "All right, you've seen some blood spilled today. Why don't you saddle up and ride?"

"If you don't want to see some more of these people shot, Britton, you'd better strap on Boone's gun and have it out with me. If you don't, I'm ordering my boys to kill every one of them."

The day he had hung up his gun, Layne Britton had known this kind of thing was going to happen. He had hoped he would be able to avoid it, but this situation left him no choice. He could not stand by and let innocent people be killed. Bill Henderson was now injured because Layne had not immediately accepted Foss's challenge.

Peeling off his coat and hanging it in a stagecoach window, the tall man said, "Since you put it that way, Pete, you've got your gunfight."

Foss laughed. "Good!"

As Boone was untying the leather thong that held his holster to his thigh, his brother said to him, "Take all the bullets out of your gun except one."

"What's this?" asked Layne, drawing near.

"Don't worry, Britton," breathed Foss. "I'll only have one bullet in my gun, too. I want all of these respectable citizens here to tell it abroad that Pete Foss went up against the great Layne Britton with only one bullet in his gun. It's only fair that you have the same limitation."

One of the passengers asked if the women could climb back in the coach so as not to see the carnage, but Foss laughed and commanded that they stay put. He wanted both the women and men to be witnesses to his outstanding feat.

Layne accepted the gunbelt from Boone Foss, buckled it on, and tied the thong to his thigh. Then he pulled the Colt .44 from its well-oiled holster, broke the action, and examined the position of the single bullet. Making sure it was in the next cylinder to come under the firing pin, he snapped it shut.

Pete Foss strutted before the witnesses, who were still under the guns of his men. He made sure they saw the single bullet in his revolver. Ozzie Gisler still knelt beside the bleeding shotgun rider, and Foss commanded Ozzie to stand up so he could see the show.

Prancing about like a ringmaster in a circus, Foss hooked his thumbs in his belt and said, "Now, I want to be sure all you good people know my name. What is it?"

When no one answered, the yellow-haired gunman bared his teeth and demanded heatedly, "What is my name?"

One of the elderly men said it softly.

"What's that?" snapped Foss. "I can't hear you!"

The man said it louder.

"That's not loud enough!" snarled Foss. "I want to hear it loud, and I want everybody to say it!"

In unison, the clustered passengers and Ozzie Gisler said, "Pete Foss."

"All right!" said Foss. "And you will remember to tell everybody in Wichita who outdrew and killed the mighty Layne Britton!" Wheeling about, he lanced Layne with his pale blue stare and said, "Okay, Britton. Let's get to it!"

As the two men spread forty feet of space between them, Layne tested the feel of the gun in the holster, lifting it and easing it down several times. Planting his feet apart, he looked at Boone Foss. "I want your word, Boone, that no matter how this goes, you'll let these people get back in the stagecoach and head for Wichita immediately. The shotgunner needs a doctor."

Boone looked at his brother.

"Give him your word," Pete Foss said emphatically.

Turning back to Layne, Boone said, "You got it."

Layne Britton nodded, then looked squarely at the thin man with the strawlike hair. Pete Foss felt the weight of Layne's penetrating steel-gray eyes, and a chill went down his spine. Ignoring this strange feeling, he rasped, "Anytime, Britton." His lips were twisted into a malignant grin. The fingers of his right hand were spread just above the gun butt.

"This is your big moment, sonny," Layne said. "Make your play."

He saw the motion in Pete Foss's eyes before the man's hand snaked downward. Layne's own hand was a blur, like the wing of a hummingbird. The Colt .44 belched fire. The bullet's impact flattened Foss. He lay on his back, a blood-ringed hole in the center of his chest. The hand that would never draw another gun was welded to the weapon, which was still in the holster.

Ozzie Gisler blinked and let out a big breath through pursed lips.

As the afternoon breeze carried away the cloud of blue-white gun smoke, Layne Britton holstered the Colt and unhitched the gunbelt. Boone Foss, his face blanched, stood unbelievingly over the lifeless form of his brother. Layne wrapped the belt around the gun and holster and slapped it against Boone Foss's flat chest. "Thanks for the use of the gun," he said quietly.

The Wells Fargo passengers stood like statues while the gang wordlessly hoisted their fallen leader's corpse across his saddle and rode away.

Ozzie Gisler's mouth hung open. As Layne shouldered into his coat, the wiry old man said, "I'd never believe it if I hadn't seen it with my own eyes!"

Speaking calmly, Layne said, "Let's put this wounded man in the coach and get him to Wichita."

Chapter Two

Pain bit at Bill Henderson as Layne and Ozzie hoisted him upward. He sucked air through his teeth but made no verbal cry. Once in the stage, the three women saw to him, one ripping up part of her petticoat to make a temporary bandage. The bullet had torn through Bill's flesh but had missed the bone.

As soon as Ozzie knew his partner was as comfortable as possible, he said with a grin, "Bill, you already got vacation time comin'. You didn't have to do this."

Bill managed to grin back, saying, "Just get up there and drive, Gisler."

Ozzie laughed. "You can't be hurt too bad. You can still smart mouth!" Backing out of the coach, he turned to Layne, who stood beside him, and said, "Mr. Britton, would you like to ride up in the box with me and Puddles?"

"Sure would," responded Layne.

Puddles wagged her short tail and let out a yip as the two men mounted the box. Layne took his seat and picked her up. "What kind of dog is she?" he asked.

Ozzie cackled. "She's purebred, Mr. Britton."

"Really?"

Taking the ribbons in his right hand, Ozzie released the brake. "Yeah. Purebred *mutt*."

Layne Britton laughed as the wiry driver snapped the reins and the Concord rolled out. Roughing the little dog's iron-gray fur, he asked, "Why did you name her Puddles?"

11

Ozzie chortled, "Now, son, if you have to ask a question like that, you ain't as smart as you look!"

Layne laughed again.

The coach settled into a steady pace, with the familiar hum of spinning wheels, rumble of hooves, and rhythmic sway. Ozzie eyed the growing shadow of the coach and team on the ground. The episode with Pete Foss had cost them nearly half an hour, but they would still be in Wichita by four-thirty, he assured himself.

"Got to hand it to you, Mr. Britton," he said. "You sure made it look like that gun leaped out of that holster right into your hand. Of course, I been hearin' stories about you for four or five years."

Layne did not comment. He calmly stroked the little dog and let his eyes roam the prairie.

Ozzie continued. "I heard about how you took out Wade Parsons up in Topeka. They say you drilled him before he could clear leather—just like I saw you do Pete Foss a little while ago. How did you get so all-fired fast?"

"Practice," replied Layne, woodenly.

"Fellow has to have some natural ability, too."

"I suppose."

"Your skill with a shootin' iron sure is talked about a lot, Mr. Britton. You're a pretty famous fellow."

Layne adjusted himself in the seat and said, "People do a lot of talking, Mr. Gisler. Sometimes they make a man out to be more than he is."

"Oh, I don't know," chuckled Ozzie. "Sometimes they're right. Take me, for instance. There's lots of folks who say I'm downright handsome and all. Now, you have to understand, Mr. Britton, it ain't that *I* think I'm good lookin', but what's my humble opinion against thousands of others?"

Layne laughed and then held the dog firmly in his lap as the stagecoach hit a hole in the road and roughly jostled its occupants. Ozzie leaned over and hollered toward the interior of the coach, "Did that bump hurt my partner?"

The answer came back that Bill Henderson was all right.

Conversation halted in the box for several minutes,

and then Ozzie said, "I've never talked to a real live gunfighter before. How does a fellow get started bein' one, anyhow?"

"Happens different ways to different men," replied Layne. "Most of them go into it for lack of purpose in life. A lot of men learned to handle revolvers in the Civil War and got to liking it. With the West full of ex-soldiers— Yankees *and* Rebels—a lot of them resolve their disputes by drawing against each other."

Ozzie Gisler nodded, interested.

"First thing you know," continued Layne, "the survivors begin to pit themselves against each other to see who is fastest and, of course, most accurate. Some men have survived numerous gunfights and, in so doing, have built reputations for themselves. Well, anytime you are king of the mountain, there is always someone who wants to take your throne."

"Like Pete Foss."

"Like Pete Foss," Layne echoed solemnly.

"Were you in the war, Mr. Britton?" asked the old driver.

"No, I wasn't, Mr. Gisler."

"Say, you don't need to call me *mister*, son," said Ozzie, grinning broadly. "I'm just plain old Ozzie Gisler."

"You started it," Layne replied.

"Just showin' respect for your talent."

Layne laughed. "Well, if respect is the thing, then I certainly owe it to you. After all, you are ten times older than I am!"

The reinsman joined Layne's laughter and cuffed him lightly on the arm. "I like you, kid," he said. "You and me could get along." After a few moments, Ozzie returned to the subject. "You weren't in the war, huh?"

"No."

"How'd you get started bein' a gunfighter?"

"It's a long story."

"We got about an hour and a half to Wichita."

Shifting position and hoisting a booted foot to the edge of the box, Layne said, "It all started down in

Austin, Texas. That's where I was born. May twelfth, 1846.''

"Well, now," put in Ozzie, "this here is 1872. September. So this last May you turned twenty-six.''

"That's right.''

"Well, *Grandpa* Britton," laughed Ozzie, "go on with your story.''

"My father was a banker in Austin," proceeded Layne. "One day almost six years ago, robbers went into Dad's bank waving their guns. After they had cleaned out the safe and the tellers' cages, they were heading out the door. One of them knocked down an elderly woman. Dad shouted angrily at him, and two of them shot him in cold blood.'' Looking at the driver's windburned face, he said, "I was angry, Mr.—er, I mean Ozzie. I got names and descriptions of the two men who killed Dad from witnesses. I vowed to hunt them down and kill them.''

"And I guess you did just that.''

"Yes, sir. I tracked them for a full year. The fast draw was the up-and-coming thing. So I practiced as I followed the trail.''

"Where'd you find them?''

"Arizona Territory. Little town of Yuma. I sought them out singly and told them who I was and what I was there for. Gave them each a chance to draw. When I killed the second one, he had a friend with him. As I started to leave, the dead man's friend put the challenge to me. We squared off, and when the smoke cleared, he was also on the ground.''

Ozzie shook his head. "Whillikers!''

Layne eyed the lowering sun. "Unfortunately that third fellow was a well-known gunfighter named Vic Mills.''

"Vic Mills!'' exclaimed Ozzie. "I knew about him. I remember when word was goin' around about him gettin' killed. Whoever it was who told me said it was some kid gun hawk who got old Vic. Well, I'll be! So it was you that outdrew him. What do you know!''

"From there it was all downhill, Ozzie," Layne said, fingering his dark mustache. "Before I left Arizona, I had to kill two more men who wanted to take on the man who had outgunned Vic Mills." Layne sighed, lowering his foot to the floor of the box. "By that time, I was what they called a famous gunfighter. I found myself living the lonely, pointless life of a drifting gunslick . . . leaving bloody bodies on saloon floors and dusty streets. Sure wasn't what I had planned for my life."

"What were you plannin' to do with yourself?" asked the bristly-faced driver.

"Be a cattle rancher. I already had a few Texas longhorns growing up on a friend's ranch. I was looking into getting a piece of land of my own when Dad got killed. By the time I could make my way back home, Mom had died. The estate had already been divided among my brothers and sisters, and my cattle had been sold. So, with empty pockets, I kept drifting. I worked on cattle ranches all over the West, but sooner or later someone would show up to challenge me, or perhaps point me out to the foreman as a gunfighter. I would get my walking papers and be on the drift again, once more a victim of the gun on my hip."

Ozzie squinted at Layne Britton's outline against the declining afternoon sun. "Well, you ain't wearin' it now. What happened? Has this trip to Wichita got somethin' to do with it?"

"Sure does." Layne nodded. "About a month ago I went to Scott City to visit an aunt—my mother's sister. She got all excited, sat me down, and told me that I was heir to a fifteen-hundred-acre ranch a few miles southwest of Wichita. Showed me official papers to prove it."

Ozzie rubbed his chin. "Fifteen hundred acres? That'd have to be Cy Kellogg's place."

"Why, yes." Layne smiled. "He was my uncle. Mom's brother. Did you know him?"

"Sure did," cackled Ozzie. "I used to have a little place not far from his. Lived there several years. Your uncle and I used to ride into the settlement when it was first begun by the Wichita Indians back in '64. I moved into town after Cy died—let's see, almost four years ago. I live over on Waco Street now, not far from the banks of the Little Arkansas."

Layne nodded. "Well, I'm glad to know you and Uncle Cyrus were friends. Anyhow, my aunt took me to her lawyer in Scott City, who looked over the papers for me. Uncle Cyrus had also left me several thousand dollars in a Wichita bank, which I was able to get through a Scott City bank."

Ozzie grinned and said, "Bought yourself some fancy new duds with some of it, I can see. Right smart outfit you got on there." Ozzie turned to shout at one of the lead horses that was being lazy. A crack of the whip over the animal's head corrected the matter. Turning his attention once again to Layne, he said, "So you're gonna be livin' on Cy's place."

"Yes, sir," said Layne. "Got enough cash to get a good herd started. Almost missed getting the place, though."

"How's that?"

"Uncle Cyrus knew I was a drifter. I was his favorite nephew, but he didn't want the place to get too run down. So he put a four-year provision in the will. If I didn't show up to claim it by the time the four years were up, the place would be sold and the money given to charity."

"When are the four years up?" asked Ozzie.

"October twenty-eighth."

"Say, you did skin it close! That's next month."

Layne nodded, smiling. "It's okay, now. We're almost to Wichita."

The aging driver pondered on it for a long moment, then asked, "Who's handlin' the legal stuff on the place?"

"When Uncle Cyrus drew up the will, it was a Wichita lawyer named Robert Catron. My aunt's attorney in Scott City told me that Catron had died some time before Uncle Cyrus. I am now to see the old man's son, Dolph, who I understand has taken over his father's practice."

At the mention of Dolph Catron's name, Ozzie Gisler's stomach turned sour. He knew Catron, Wichita's leading attorney and land developer, to be money hungry and unscrupulous. Ozzie was convinced he would stop at nothing to enlarge his fortune. Most of the people in Wichita, however, believed him to be a man of honesty and integrity.

"Do you know Mr. Catron?" asked Layne.

"Oh, uh . . . yes. Yes, I know him," Ozzie replied, masking his true feelings. He wanted to tell Layne what he thought of Dolph Catron, but this was none of his business. In any case, it was a month before the deadline, so the Kellogg place was already Layne's property. All he had to do was walk in and claim it.

"The lawyer in Scott City said Catron's the richest man in Wichita."

"I reckon that's so." Ozzie nodded. "So you hung up your gun when you knew you had a place of your own?" he asked, changing the subject.

"Sure did." Layne smiled. "Now I'm my own boss, so nobody can fire me if they find out I used to be a gunslinger."

"From what happened today with Pete Foss, I would say you're still gonna have some problems with greenhorn hopefuls."

Layne took a deep breath. "Afraid so. I'll just have to outlast it. A few years and there'll be enough gun hawks to take my place. Then my name won't mean anything."

"You gonna go by Adam Britton in Wichita? I mean, that's how you signed on this coach at Dodge City."

"I'm going to try," said the ex-gunfighter. "Adam is my middle name, so there's nothing dishonest about it."

"Probably won't work," said Ozzie. "Too many people know your face."

Layne shrugged his shoulders. "I'll give it a try. All I can do."

Ozzie grinned, saying, "All the luck in the world to you, son."

"Thanks. I'm going to need it."

Layne Britton swept the broad prairie with his steel-gray eyes. The land lay flat, broken by an occasional low bluff and by erratic gullies. In places there were shallow streams, usually lined with trees. The rich green grass, spotted with yellow patches, swayed under soft breezes that played haphazardly across the open fields.

Ozzie Gisler suddenly pointed eastward and shouted, "There she is!"

Layne's gaze followed the driver's crooked finger. He

could just make out the outline of the town of Wichita,
lying on the horizon. He was glad to see it. A brand-new
chapter of his life would begin here. As the rocking,
swaying stagecoach pulled him nearer, the ex-gunfighter
felt a chill of exhilaration. Uncle Cyrus's generosity had
changed the whole prospect for his future.

Thirty minutes passed. As the Concord lifted onto the
crest of a gentle rise, the golden sunlight flared across the
surface of the Arkansas and the Little Arkansas rivers. The
rivers resembled two copper-colored ribbons flowing lan-
guidly across the vast prairie, coming together in a splen-
did bow at the northwest edge of Wichita, Layne Britton's
new home.

Traveling to Wichita from the west was made much
simpler earlier that year by the completion in July 1872 of
a bridge that spanned the Arkansas River. The bridge led
in on Douglas Avenue, which became the hub of com-
merce in town. Also completed that year was a railroad
from Wichita that connected with the main line, the Santa
Fe, at Newton. This railroad transported over seventy
thousand head of cattle the year it was built. Layne Britton
would find his new home to be prospering both as a cattle
town and as a burgeoning trade center.

Ozzie Gisler swung his bright red Concord stagecoach
onto the dusty road that led to the bridge. Off to the right
lay the town cemetery, nestled among a stand of towering
cottonwood trees and surrounded by a waist-high white
picket fence. The horses whinnied at the humid scent of
the river in the distance as the coach approached the
cemetery.

When the leather-faced driver saw several buggies
clustered at the gate of the cemetery, he slowed the team
in respect. A large, somber crowd was gathered around a
mound of earth and an open grave. A coffin hovered over
the yawning hole, waiting to be lowered into the sod.

Ozzie's line of sight focused on the stiff features of
Dolph Catron, who stood, hat in hand, facing the road.
Next to Catron's bulky frame stood a slender feminine

form, shoulders drooped, her lovely face and dark hair obscured by a black veil.

Ozzie mumbled a name. "Cora."

Pulling his gaze from the crowd in the cemetery, Layne asked, "What's that, Ozzie?"

"Oh, I said Cora. Cora Catron."

"Catron?"

"Yes. Your lawyer Dolph Catron's wife. She's had tuberculosis for about three years. That stout fellow next to the grave is Dolph. Cora's been expected to go anytime." Shaking his head, Ozzie added, "Poor little Connie."

"Connie?"

"Cora's daughter. That's her standin' there by Dolph. Prettiest little thing in Wichita. Twenty years old. Cheated herself out of havin' sweethearts and good times to be at her mother's bedside these past three years."

Layne saw the young woman named Connie turn away from the dismal coffin as it hovered over the yawning grave. The minister's voice carried across the cemetery, speaking words of comfort. Briefly the young woman's attention was drawn to the dusty road as Ozzie Gisler's bright red stagecoach rolled slowly by, then she again bowed her head.

Rumbling past the cemetery, the stage team pulled the Wells Fargo coach onto the bridge. Clucking his tongue, Ozzie said, "When Connie was fourteen, her pa ran off and left them. Just up and skipped town, like he didn't care nothin' about neither one of 'em."

"Another woman?" asked Layne.

"No, sir. That's the funny thing about it. Morgan Lee had been a colonel in the Union Army in the war. Got out of the army after the war so he could be with his wife and daughter. Took a job as Sedgwick County surveyor. Then all of a sudden, like a bunch of mad hornets was on his tail, he just up and took off. Went right back and rejoined the army. Don't make a lick of sense. He's commandant at Fort Dodge, now. They tell me he ain't never got married again, neither. Ain't even got a girlfriend."

"That sure doesn't add up, Ozzie."

"No, it doesn't. And on top of that, when Morgan up

and left he never even told that sweet little daughter of his good-bye. Broke her little heart all to pieces. Been six years, now, and he ain't never sent her one letter. Nary a one. When Connie found out he was at Fort Dodge, she wrote her daddy a blisterin' letter. Told him off good.''

"Sounds like he had it coming," mused Layne.

"That he did—and I should know. You see, me and Connie are real close. She tells me all her troubles. Dolph Catron's never even tried to be a dad to her, and since her real dad deserted her, she sort of adopted me. Calls me Uncle Ozzie. And every time I come in off a run, that gorgeous creature gives old Uncle Ozzie a big hug and kiss." The driver grinned. "You just wait till you get a look at that pretty gal. Take it from old Ozzie, son. That woman's a beauty!"

The dust-covered coach moved eastward down Douglas Avenue and made a left turn on North Main. The Wells Fargo office was in the next block, just past First Street, with Dr. Manley Wilson's office directly across the street. Rolling to a stop, Ozzie set the brake and spoke to the Wells Fargo agent as he emerged from the door.

"Guess you saw the crowd at the cemetery," the agent said. "Cora Catron."

"Yeah," said the driver, climbing down. "I saw."

Layne Britton and Ozzie Gisler carried Bill Henderson across the street and placed him on one of the cots in Doc Wilson's office. The doctor was attending Cora Catron's funeral, and Ozzie told Layne that he would stay with Bill until Wilson was summoned from the cemetery.

Layne bent down to Bill, lying on his cot, and said, "I'm sorry you were shot on my account, Mr. Henderson. It was needless violence, and it shouldn't have happened."

"Oh, no, Mr. Britton. It was my own fault. I should have kept my mouth shut."

"I just wish it hadn't happened." Layne sighed. Turning to Ozzie, he asked, "Do you think I have time to ride out and look at the Kellogg place before dark?"

"Sure. You can put the horse to a trot and be out there in less than an hour. Doesn't get dark this time of year till about seven, seven-thirty. Livery stable is just a block over on Market."

"How do I get out to the ranch?"

"Simple," responded the old driver. "Just ride Market Street all the way out of town until you reach a road headin' west. There's an old hay sweep sittin' right there all rusted up. That's Kellogg Road. Just ride west till the road runs out, and you'll be on your new property."

"Thanks," said Layne. "Guess that Sunflower Hotel we just passed on Douglas is okay, isn't it?"

"Sure is, son. I'd invite you to come stay at my place till you get settled at the ranch, but I only got one bed. Puddles sleeps with me. I'm afraid it would be a mite uncomfortable for the three of us."

"That's okay, Ozzie." Layne smiled. As he started to turn away, he paused and added, "I won't bother Dolph Catron until tomorrow, but where's his office?"

"Just two doors up, son. This same side of the street."

"Much obliged," said Layne. "See you later."

Layne Britton picked up his gear, then headed for the Sunflower Hotel. Entering the lobby, he stepped around a teenage boy who was sweeping the floor. A middle-aged man sat in an overstuffed chair reading a newspaper. Behind the desk stood a thin, bald-headed man with wire-framed glasses that perched on the end of his nose.

The clerk eyed Layne's expensive outfit, smiled, and said, "Good evening, sir. May I help you?"

"I need a room," Layne replied, smiling back.

"Just so happens we've been saving one for someone just like you," said the clerk in a friendly manner. Pushing the register toward Layne and handing him a freshly dipped pen, he asked, "How long will you be staying with us?"

"It'll probably be something like a week."

"That's fine, sir. The room is two dollars a day."

As he signed the register, Layne asked, "Do you want it in advance?"

Over his spectacles, the clerk studied Layne's clothes another time. "Ah . . . no, sir," he said. "That won't be necessary."

Layne handed him back the pen in exchange for a door key.

"Room seven, upstairs, sir. Overlooks the street."

"Fine," said Layne, picking up his gear.

"I hope you'll enjoy your stay with us . . . Mr. . . . ." Dropping his eyes to the register, the clerk raised them again. "Mr. Britton. Adam Britton. Say, are you any relation to *Layne* Britton?"

The man in the overstuffed chair looked up, then dropped his newspaper. Bounding past the busy sweep boy, he spoke before the tall man could answer, "Related to him, nothing! Fred, this *is* Layne Britton!"

Layne's heart sank.

Extending his hand, the man said, "My name is Chester Higgins, Mr. Britton."

Layne set down the suitcase and clasped Higgins's hand.

Bubbling with excitement, Higgins said to the wide-eyed clerk, "Fred, I saw this man up in Omaha! There were three gun hawks challenging him right in the middle of the street. Layne—I mean, Mr. Britton—drew his gun faster than a rattler's tongue. One man died at his feet, a bullet through his heart. Mr. Britton flattened himself in the dust, making the other two miss. Then he rolled and fired, dropping both of them. Mr. Britton left them all dead in the street and walked away through a cloud of gun smoke!"

By this time, the fourteen-year-old sweep boy, Danny Smith, was standing in the middle of the lobby. His mouth hung open. "Hey, mister," he said, "are you really Layne Britton?"

Layne sighed and turned to the tall and gangly youth. "Yes. I'm him." Looking at the clerk, he added, "We'll just leave it Adam in the register. It's my middle name."

"Yes, sir, Mr. Britton," agreed the clerk.

Picking up his bags, Layne said, "Nice to have met you, Mr. Higgins." With that, he ascended the stairs.

Instantly, Danny Smith leaned his broom against the wall, and called out, "Fred, I'll be back in a few minutes." He dashed out the door as the clerk stood shaking his head.

* * *

Boone Foss's favorite hangout was the Broken Spur Saloon on the corner of Douglas Avenue and Main Street, a few doors up from the Sunflower Hotel, and that was where he headed after delivering his brother's body to the undertaker. He was seated now at a table in the saloon, playing poker and nursing his anger and depression with a bottle of whiskey. At the moment he was locked in a duel of wits with an older man, while four other men who had started in the game and quit looked on with special interest. The mound of wrinkled greenbacks and gold coins in front of Boone dwarfed the small amount in front of the other man. A sizable pile of bills and coins made up the pot in the center of the table.

Boone Foss had a craggy face and hawklike nose. His hazel eyes were set close together. The lid of the left one drooped, giving him a malignant appearance. "Did you say you were calling me, Harold?" asked Boone, his homely features expressionless.

"Yes," replied Harold Noyes, his own face set in hard lines.

Boone casually fanned his cards faceup on the table. Noyes eyed them carefully, then slammed his own cards facedown in disgust. The crowd of men laughed and congratulated Boone as he raked the pot to himself. Noyes sat glumly in his chair as the young gun hawk pulled a ready-made cigarette from a shirt pocket. Thumbing a match into flame, Boone lit the cigarette, waved out the match, and dropped its smoking remains in his empty shot glass.

By now Harold Noyes's eyes glittered like burning coal against his sagging, weathered skin. With words cut short and brittle, he spattered, "Foss, you cheated me."

Boone Foss's attention sharpened on the man. He stood up, knocking his chair backward with the back of his leg. All eyes in the place were riveted on Boone, who stood glaring down at Noyes, his eyes narrowed. "I'd like for you to repeat that," he said, gravel in his voice.

The smoke-filled air of the room was tight with

hostility. Staying in the chair, Harold Noyes said, "You couldn't have come up with that hand, Foss. You cheated me."

Boone stepped forward, placed his palms flat on the table, and bent toward the older man, his evil eyes honed to sharp points. "Harold, you will have to back up your accusation out in the street."

Suddenly Noyes realized he had let his temper push him into a dangerous situation. His features went slack. "Oh no, you don't," he said, running his words together. "I'm not drawin' against you!"

Anger bolted through Boone Foss. He flung the table savagely across the room, scattering money, glasses, and whiskey bottles. Backing up, he took his stance, splayed hands hovering over his hips. "On your feet, Noyes!" he bellowed. "Go for your gun!"

The men in the room retreated, making sure they were out of the line of fire.

Harold Noyes's stomach tightened into a hard, cold ball. A prickly feeling ran up the back of his neck. Keeping his hands away from the gun on his hip, he stammered, "N-no, Boone. I . . . I ain't d-drawin' against you."

"If I thought a man cheated me," said Boone, "I'd welcome the chance to put a bullet in him."

"I . . . I'm sorry," squeaked Noyes, swallowing hard. "I w-was wrong."

"You'll either draw against me or crawl out of here on your hands and knees," Boone said through his teeth.

Relief spread on Noyes's pallid face. "I'll c-crawl, Boone."

The crowd of men laughed as Harold Noyes went to his hands and knees and began to crawl toward the saloon doors. Just as he reached the doors, young Danny Smith charged through, stumbling over him. There was more laughter as the youth rolled and slammed against a table. Harold Noyes took advantage of the moment to hurry out the door.

Danny got up, dusting himself, and said, "Boone, I gotta talk to you."

Boone took a deep puff on his cigarette as the men in

the saloon began congratulating him. "I'm buyin' drinks for everyone!" he said, ignoring the boy.

Stepping closer, Danny spoke emphatically, "Boone, I gotta tell you something."

"Later, kid," he replied, brushing at him like he would a pesky fly. "C'mon, men! Bottoms up!"

The gunfighter turned toward the bar. From behind he heard Danny Smith say loudly, "Boone, Layne Britton is in town!"

Boone Foss froze in his tracks. Every voice went still. No one had had the courage to mention Layne Britton's name since Boone's older brother, Pete, had been shot.

Slowly, Boone turned, pulled the cigarette from his lips, and smiled. "Come here, kid," he said, motioning him to a corner.

"Yes, sir!" the youth eagerly replied, following him to a secluded table.

Danny Smith was an orphan, and he lived in a small room at the back of the Sunflower Hotel, earning his keep by cleaning and doing odd jobs for the hotel. With no father to guide him, Danny had begun to fill his need for paternal leadership with twenty-year-old Boone Foss. Like Danny, who had an ever-tousled shock of blond hair, Boone was slender and blond, and Danny admired the way he wore his Colt .44 slung low on his hips and thonged to his thigh. He admired even more the way Boone boasted of having already outdrawn and killed two men, with his brother laying claim to killing four. Knowing that Danny idolized him, Boone would occasionally spend time with him, letting the lad practice with Boone's Colt.

Danny had often heard the Foss brothers mention Layne Britton, and Boone once told him that his big goal in life was to take on the eminent gunslinger—if his brother didn't kill him first. So when Danny had learned Layne was at the Sunflower Hotel, he knew Boone would want to know.

"Danny," Boone asked as they sat down, "where did you see Layne Britton?"

"He just registered at the hotel. I thought you and Pete would be interested."

Boone's expression grew hard at the mention of his brother, but then his features relaxed. "I know all about Layne. We ran into him out on the stage road, and Pete braced him."

"Really?" Danny's eyes grew wide. "What happened?"

"Well, Britton's walking around town and Pete isn't. He's over at the undertaker's." As Danny's jaw dropped, Boone continued. "Yes, I already saw Mr. Layne Britton in action—and he's fast. But I'm faster."

With the light dancing back into his eyes, Danny asked, "You gonna brace him, Boone?"

"You have any idea how long he's plannin' to be in town, kid?"

"He told Fred he'd be here about a week. You're gonna brace him, aren't you?"

Every eye in the room was fixed on the impassive mold of Boone Foss's face.

"Sure am, kid," said Boone, tight lipped. "I owe him for killing my brother. They might as well go ahead and dig Layne Britton's grave right now, because I'm gonna put him in it."

"Hey!" shouted one of the men. "I'll drink to that! Let's all drink to Boone Foss's bullet—the one that's gonna put Layne Britton in his grave!"

Chapter Three

At the close of the prayer at the cemetery, Connie Lee, standing beside her stepfather, saw the four men grasp the ropes that suspended the coffin. The woman's heart felt like hot lead as she watched the oblong box being lowered into the unfeeling earth.

No one could know the bitterness or the profound sadness that claimed the raven-haired beauty at that moment, nor could anyone know the rampant hostile thoughts that battered her mind. The minister's words filtered into her thinking as he tossed a handful of dirt on the coffin, saying, "Ashes to ashes, dust to dust."

The crowd of mourners stood immobile until the man with the Bible in his hand had gone to Connie and her stepfather and offered personal words of solace. Slowly, then, the mourners filed by to give their condolences. A quarter-hour had expired by the time the last person stepped away.

The bitterness in Connie's heart remained under constraint until Dolph Catron cupped a hand on her shoulder and said, "Let's go, Connie."

The woman jerked away as if she had been touched with a red-hot iron. Despite the veil, Catron could see the savage fury in her eyes. His face lost color as she hissed, "Don't you touch me! Never! Do you hear? Don't you ever touch me!"

Nervously, Dolph Catron threw a glance at the last

few people climbing into their vehicles. Some had heard
Connie's outburst and were turning around to look. "Keep
your voice down!" he said in a hoarse whisper.

"Why?" she said loudly. "Are you afraid someone
will find out what you really are?" Wheeling, she started
toward the gate. Catron seized her arm and spun her
around. Baring her teeth, she whipped her arm from his
grip and snapped, "I told you not to touch me!"

"Connie," Dolph said, whispering, "what's come
over you? Why are you acting like this?"

"Mother told me the truth before she died."

The angry woman walked to the surrey and climbed
in, leaving Dolph Catron to digest her words. Several of
the vehicles had not yet pulled away, and the occupants
were sitting and staring. One of the men called, "Miss
Connie! Is something wrong?"

"It's all right, Mr. Walker," she called back. "You
folks can go on home now."

Catron paused beside the surrey to light a cigar, then
climbed in beside his stepdaughter and grasped the reins.
Connie sat stiff and sullen as the surrey moved out. The
other vehicles fell in behind, the occupants talking among
themselves. As the surrey moved slowly toward town,
Connie stared absently at the passing countryside, her
mind drifting back to her childhood, back to early summer,
1866.

The week after school had let out, Connie had gone
with a schoolmate, Alice Barnes, and her family to Salina
for ten days. When she returned home, she dashed into the
house, anxious to tell her mother of her trip.

Connie found her mother behind the house, pruning a
rose bush. She ran to her mother, and the two embraced.
Cora Lee was a small woman with coal-black hair and
dark-brown eyes. The dark-haired fourteen-year-old daughter bore a strong resemblance to her mother, but had
inherited her father's green eyes. It was evident that the
girl was going to be a very becoming woman.

"Did you have a good time, darling?" asked Cora.

"Oh, yes, Mother!" exclaimed the girl. "But I'm

going to make you wait until Daddy gets home, then I can tell you both at the same time."

Cora Lee's eyes dulled. Her face pinched.

"What's wrong, Mother?" asked Connie.

With shaky hands, Cora guided her daughter toward the house, saying, "Let's go inside, dear. I have something I need to talk to you about."

Reading her mother's harrowed expression, Connie said, "Has something happened to Daddy?"

Passing through the door, Cora said, "No, honey. Not . . . not exactly."

"What do you mean, *not exactly*, Mother?" asked Connie, fear rising within her.

Going to the kitchen table, Cora sat down. Connie stood over her. "Mother, what's happened to Daddy?"

"Honey," said Cora, looking her daughter straight in the eye, "your father has left us."

"Left us? What do you mean?"

"He's gone, Connie. He quit his job with the county. He simply came home one day last week and told me he was leaving. I asked him why. He said he didn't want to be married to me anymore."

Connie was totally stunned. Her mouth worked, but no sound would come.

Continuing, Cora said, "I asked your father where he was going. He wouldn't tell me. I asked him what was going to happen to you and me. Connie, he said that he didn't care what happened to us."

Tears were spilling down the girl's cheeks. Finding her voice, she stammered, "He . . . he d-doesn't care?"

"That's what he said."

Connie was crushed. She had been very close to her father, and she couldn't understand how he could leave. She would never believe he didn't love them.

Cora went on to explain that since Morgan Lee wanted to be shed of them, she was going to divorce him. She had already gone to Dolph Catron, the attorney, who was handling it for her.

At first, the pain the girl felt was overwhelming. She was tortured when she tried to imagine that her father did not love her. She wondered how he could have been so convincing . . . how he could have taken her in his arms, as he had countless times, and told her that he loved her.

In retaliation for the hurt so deep within her, she tried to hate him. She soon learned that it just was not in her to hate her own father. But anger was there—seething, burning anger that would not go away.

One day, months after this shattering news, when Connie came home from school, Cora said, "Mr. Catron was by today, dear."

"Oh?"

"He found out where your father is. The papers for the divorce will be served to him shortly."

"Where is he, Mother?" Connie asked, trying to appear only slightly interested.

"Well, he has rejoined the army. They gave him the rank of colonel back. He is now commandant at Fort Dodge."

"Fort Dodge?" echoed the girl. "So close?"

Dolph Catron's report of the whereabouts of Morgan Lee renewed the pain in Connie's heart and rekindled the flame of anger within her. That very night, she sat down at the desk in her room. Taking pen in hand, she wrote:

Colonel Lee,

Having just today learned of your physical location, I have decided to write you and express my feelings. Since my darling mother has raised me to be a lady, I do not use cuss words. So I may not be able to say exactly what I feel. But I will try.

I think you are the most wicked, evil man in the world. I hope nobody ever loves you or is nice to you. I hope you never have another happy day in your whole life. Don't expect me to cry at your funeral, because I would not even come to it.

Be sure you understand this. I mean it. I never ever want to see you again. Good-bye forever.

                                   Cora Lee's daughter,
                                   Connie Lee

After the divorce was final, Dolph Catron began to appear frequently at the house. Twice Connie had inadvertently walked in on her mother and the lawyer when they were kissing. Connie was not terribly fond of Catron, but he seemed to be giving Cora the love that Morgan Lee had failed to give, so she accepted him. After several months, the happy couple told Connie of their wedding plans.

The settlement begun by the Wichita Indians was growing, and more white men were moving in. A real town was developing. Dolph Catron was going to build the biggest, most luxurious house in Wichita for his new bride and stepdaughter.

The wedding had taken place exactly one week after the house was finished, when Connie was fifteen. Cora Lee became Mrs. Dolph Catron, wife of Wichita's leading land developer and most prominent attorney, having taken over his father's successful practice following his recent death.

The Catrons had been married little more than a year when Cora came down with tuberculosis. The doctor had suggested that Cora be moved to a higher, drier climate, such as the mountains of Colorado, but Dolph had argued that there were not enough people there for him to make a living at either of his professions. The Catrons stayed in Wichita. Dolph grew richer, and Cora grew sicker.

In devotion to her dying mother, Connie seldom left Cora's side. Dolph had offered to hire a cook and housekeeper, but Connie told him that she wanted to do everything herself for her mother as long as she lived.

Often young men came to court the beautiful woman and invite her to barn dances and other social functions. But each time, Connie refused, choosing to spend every waking moment with her mother.

A cold chill slithered down Connie's spine now as she

rode in the surrey, smelling Dolph Catron's cigar and reliving the events of just three nights ago. . . .

As Connie had administered Cora's nightly medicine, the dying woman had asked, "Connie, did Dolph leave for the community meeting yet?"

"Yes, Mother," she replied, "about twenty minutes ago."

Cora coughed into the fresh handkerchief Connie had just supplied. She tried to speak but was taken with a severe spasm. Connie looked at her mother with pity. Her dark hair, once so pretty, was now dull and matted. Her face was pale and drawn, with dark circles around hollow eyes that didn't seem to focus on anything.

When the coughing spell was over, Cora patted the bed beside her and said, "Come. Sit down. I must talk with you."

Connie settled on the bed and took Cora's hand in her own. She could read anguish in her mother's eyes, anguish that went beyond the physical torment that wracked her frail body. "What is it, Mother?" she asked, a slight tremor in her voice.

Tears surfaced in Cora's eyes. Beginning slowly, she said, "Connie, we both know that I will be dead very soon."

Connie's face pinched. "Please, Mother—"

"We must face it," cut in Cora. "Connie, you have been so good to me. No mother ever had a daughter as sweet and unselfish as you. I know the sacrifices you have made to be with me constantly for these three years. I owe you so much."

"Mother, dear, you don't owe me anything," said Connie, forcing a smile and squeezing Cora's hand. "I have done it because I love you."

Cora Catron bit down hard on her lower lip. The tears were spilling now onto her sunken cheeks. Connie dabbed at the tears with a handkerchief. Gaining a degree of control, her trembling mother said, "Darling, there is something I must tell you before I die. It may make you hate me, but I cannot die with this thing eating at my conscience."

Tenderly, Connie said, "Mother, there is nothing that could ever make me hate you. What on earth could—"

Cutting in again, the dying woman said with difficulty, "Connie, I have wronged you beyond description. I have also wronged your father."

Confusion furrowed Connie's finely formed brow. "Me? My father? You have wronged us? How?"

Swallowing hard and fighting to maintain control, Cora said, "Let me start at the beginning. About eight months before your father left, I . . . I started having an affair with Dolph Catron."

Connie felt as if she had been hit in the stomach with a battering ram. As calmly as possible she said, "Go on."

Cora cleared her throat. "Dolph had money and the means to provide luxuries I could never have known being married to a land surveyor. I—I thought I had fallen in love with him. I know now that I had fallen in love with his money."

Connie's mother felt the deep penetration of her daughter's eyes. Continuing, she said, "We had to sneak around to have our times together. We felt it was worth it, because we imagined that we were so madly in love. Dolph began to pressure me to tell your father of our affair. There could then be a divorce, and Dolph and I could have each other. I wouldn't hear of it because of what it would do to you and to the relationship between you and me."

Connie found speech difficult. Choking out the words, she said, "Go on."

"Well . . . while you were in Salina, there was a day when your father was supposed to be out surveying some land several miles east of here. Circumstances brought him home early." Cora cleared her throat again. "When . . . when he came in unexpectedly . . . well . . . there we were. Caught red-handed."

Connie's fingers were unwittingly bearing down on the trembling hand of her mother.

Cora proceeded. "Right there on the spot, I told your father that Dolph and I were in love. I told him I was tired of living on a surveyor's wages, and that I wanted a divorce. I was going to marry Dolph. Your father was ready to tear Dolph apart with his bare hands. He kept enough control that he just ordered him out of the house.''

Connie's heart was pounding within her breast like a hammer. She said nothing.

"Your father and I sat up and talked all night," continued Cora. "He tried to talk sense into my head, but I wouldn't listen. When I finally convinced him that what I had felt for him was gone, and he saw I was bent on the divorce, he said he would take you and leave Wichita. Dolph and I could have each other, and he would build a new life for you.''

The young woman's facial features began to pinch.

"Your father loves you, Connie. He loves you very much.''

Tears misted Connie's eyes as she said, "Then why did he just take off like he did? Why didn't he at least leave me a letter? Why—"

"Let me go on," said Cora. "Those questions will be thoroughly answered in a moment." Cora took a deep breath, then continued. "When your father spoke of taking you with him, I asked where he was going to go and what he was going to do. When he said he didn't know, I talked hard and persuaded him that you would be better provided for under my care. He might drift from place to place for some time before he could settle down. That would be bad for a fourteen-year-old girl. He had to agree I was right.''

Connie was feeling cold inside.

"I promised him," said Cora, "that Dolph and I would be discreet. We would wait a respectable length of time before getting married. There would be no scandal to mar his daughter's life. He also . . .''

At this point, Cora broke down. It took several minutes to regain her composure. She coughed heavily, then wiping tears, said, "This is the part of which I am ashamed the most, Connie.''

Connie looked solemnly at the dying woman and said, "He also *what*, Mother?''

"He . . . he also . . . he also made me promise that

when he got settled, you could come and visit him as
much as you desired.''

Connie's hand flew to her mouth. Wide eyed and
tearful, she cried, ''You mean he did want to see me? He
did want me with him?''

Cora's face contorted with guilt and shame. ''Yes,
honey, he did.''

Working at controlling her emotions, Connie asked,
''But why did I never hear from him? Why hasn't he
contacted me?''

The dying woman's body shook as she replied, ''He
left you a letter when he moved away. I was to give it to
you when you came home from Salina.''

Connie's lips quivered. ''Where is my letter, Mother?''

''I—I burned it, honey.''

Connie's features tightened. ''You had no right to do
that! Why did you tell me that Daddy didn't love me?
Didn't want me? Why, Mother? Why?''

''Because . . . because if I had let you see him, you
would have found out about my infidelity with Dolph. You
would have turned away from me! I couldn't have stood
that, Connie. I love you too much!''

Levelly, Connie said, ''You loved me so much that
you let me despise my father for something he didn't do.
You so perverted my thinking toward him that I . . . I . . .
oh, dear God . . . I wrote him that awful letter!'' Connie
broke into tears, sobbing heavily.

As her sobbing eased, Cora said, ''There is more I
must tell you, Connie.''

Looking through swollen, reddened eyes, the heartbro-
ken young woman waited.

''Not long after he had left, a letter came to you from
your father. Dolph just happened to pick up the mail that
day at the Wells Fargo office. He saw the letter and
brought it to me. I burned it, also.''

Connie Lee sat numbly on the bed beside her mother.
The words she was hearing seemed to come from somewhere far off.

Cora went on. ''Dolph went to Harry Dunn at the
Fargo office and told him to intercept any letters that came

to you from Morgan Lee, explaining that the letters would upset you. Harry was to give them to Dolph. Many letters came, and they were all burned.''

"Oh, Mother!" gasped Connie.

As if getting the truth out was relieving much inward pain, Cora hastened to finish. "Your father sent you several telegrams, too. Dolph also intercepted those. Many of the letters had money in them, Connie. The money was for stagecoach fare, so you could go see him. Then, all of a sudden, the letters and telegrams stopped coming."

"Then you knew where he was before he became commander of Fort Dodge?''

"Yes. We knew that you understood he had to be found and served the papers before the divorce could be finalized. Dolph had actually taken care of it immediately after the first letter came for you. We were simply allowing for that socially approved amount of time to pass before getting married. We held off as long as we thought wise before telling you where your father was."

"Mother," said Connie cautiously, "when did the letters and telegrams stop coming from Daddy?''

Cora's face was a spectral mask of torment. "When . . . when you wrote him that letter.''

Guilt pierced Connie's heart as the words of the letter, written so long ago, echoed through her mind, taunting her mercilessly. Ejecting a long, shrill wail, she leaped from the bed, crying, "Oh, Daddy! Oh, my poor father! What have I done? What have I done?''

Cora Catron seemed to grow smaller, lying there against the large white pillow. Her face twisted as she said, "Please, Connie! Connie, darling! Don't hate me. Please don't hate me.''

The dark-haired young woman stood over her mother like a cold stone statue. An iron impassivity washed over her features. Tonelessly, she said, "I don't hate you, Mother. I said nothing could make me hate you. I will always love you. But do you realize what you have caused me to do to the only man in this world who ever loved me, besides Uncle Ozzie? Now he'll never want to see me again!''

Cora coughed and said, "I couldn't die without tell-
ing you, honey. I was wrong. Totally wrong. I know that.
You have every right to hate me. But I beg of you,
Connie, please. Please don't hate me!"

Connie's features relaxed slightly. Stepping slowly to
the bed, she kissed Cora's forehead. "I don't hate you,
Mother," she said, still with little tone in her voice. "I
love you. Now I must go to my room."

As Connie passed through the door, moving like a
sleepwalker, the sound of Dolph returning home carried up
the stairs. Entering her room, the devastated young woman
closed the door, flung herself on the bed, and wept.

Connie had no idea how much time had elapsed when
a heavy masculine voice from the hallway caught her
attention. Straining her ears, she recognized the voice to
be that of Doc Wilson. She had barely put her feet on the
floor when there came a knock on the door, followed by
the voice of Dolph Catron. "Connie. It's your mother.
You'd better come!"

Flinging open the door, Connie dashed to her mother's
room, passing Catron in the hallway. Doc Wilson stood by
the bed, bending over Cora. Looking past his shoulder, he
focused on Connie and slowly shook his head.

Straightening, the physician stepped back, allowing
Connie to move close. A glassy stare was in the dying
woman's eyes, and a gray-white pallor blanched her face.

Dolph Catron stood in the doorway. He could not
distinguish his wife's words when she fixed her languid
eyes on Connie and half whispered, "Please forgive me."

Whispering back, Connie said, "Yes, Mother. I forgive you."

A faint smile curved Cora's colorless lips, and then
she was gone.

At the Sunflower Hotel Layne Britton climbed the
stairs and found room number seven. Then he began to
unpack. He washed and changed into jeans, then stepped
back into the hall, locked the door, and pocketed the key.
Descending the stairs, he crossed the lobby under the close

inspection of Chester Higgins and a man who sat with him. The clerk was not in sight.

Following Ozzie Gisler's directions, the tall man walked through the long shadows of the buildings to the livery stable on Market Street. He picked out a lively bay mare, saddled her, and rode southwest toward Douglas Avenue. As he gained the corner, a long string of horses, buggies, surreys, and wagons was filing by. The mourners were returning from the cemetery.

The tall man's gaze settled on a feminine form dressed in black, riding in a fancy, expensive surrey. She was seated next to the stocky man that Ozzie Gisler had pointed out as Dolph Catron. Smoke from Catron's cigar was drifting past the woman's veiled face. Layne wondered if Connie Lee was really as beautiful as Ozzie claimed.

When the last vehicle in the long procession had passed, Layne nudged his mare and headed west out of town. He was unaware of the narrow pair of eyes that watched him until he faded from view.

Boone Foss stood outside the saloon, palm resting on the handle of his gun, a cold, sardonic smile etched on his face.

Chapter Four

Layne Britton put the frisky bay mare to a trot as he crossed Douglas Avenue and left Wichita behind. The sun was nearing the western horizon. Layne did not mind the thought of returning to town in the dark, but he wanted to arrive at the ranch with enough light left for him to give the place a good going over. His plan was to see Dolph Catron in the morning and clear up the necessary legal details. Then, having already seen what materials were needed at the ranch, he would purchase them, rent a wagon, and begin work on the place.

Layne's eyes were fixed straight ahead, looking for the rusty old hay sweep that Ozzie said would be his landmark. He had just spotted the rake, half buried in a patch of weeds, when off to his left he saw a band of at least a dozen riders approaching, headed for Wichita.

As Layne drew near Kellogg Road, the riders met him. Suddenly he realized that he recognized a few of the men as having been with the Foss brothers when they had halted the stagecoach. Then his line of sight zeroed in on the hard features of the leader. It was a face he knew.

The leader raised his hand military style, bringing the band to a halt. The evening breeze carried away the dust raised by the rumbling hooves.

"Howdy, Layne," said the leader. "Been a long time."

There was no smile on Layne Britton's lips as he nodded and said, "Guess you're right, Cole. It *has* been a spell."

Cole Clinger was an outlaw of the basest sort. He was a tough, rawboned man of fifty. He was clean shaven but wore his graying hair long at the back so that it dangled over his sweat-stained collar. Clinger was inordinately homely, with a sharp hatchet face dominated by a pair of dark, piercing eyes. He was a man who projected calm self-assurance and a conviction that he could do anything he pleased.

The riders studied the tall, clean-cut man on the bay mare as Clinger said slowly, "Guess it was St. Joe, wasn't it?"

"Sounds right," Layne replied.

"One of my men, here, was telling me how easy you sent Pete to meet his maker today."

"He was a mite slow," said Layne, shifting his steel-gray gaze to the group of riders, then bringing it back to Clinger.

"I warned him when he rode out this morning that they'd bring him back feet first," said the hatchet-faced man. "Can't tell these fool kids anything these days. Soon as he received word you were on that stage, he got ants in his pants. Couldn't even wait till you got to town. He'd killed himself a couple of worn-out gunfighters who had arthritic hands. Puffed up bigger than a balloon. I told him of some of the gunslicks I've watched you take out. He figured maybe you'd slowed some." Cole Clinger eyed the man on the bay mare warily. "Did you really hang up your gun, Layne?"

"Yes, I did, Cole."

"What're you doing in Wichita?" Clinger asked.

"Business."

One of the horses stamped and blew as Clinger said, "Why don't you throw in with me? You could add a little class to this bunch."

"All of these are your boys?" asked Layne.

"Yeah. The ones you saw with Pete today just went along to see the show." Clinger pulled a slim cigarillo from a shirt pocket and put it between his lips. Fishing in another pocket for a match, he said, "I'll repeat my offer, Layne. How about throwing in with me? With the railroad coming this way, we've got some big plans in the making. You could make yourself a wad.''

"You've got a bad memory, Cole," Layne said through tight lips. "When you made your offer three years ago in St. Joseph, I told you that although I was a gunfighter, I was not an outlaw.''

"Outlawing pays better than the thirty dollars a month you'd make punching cattle," said Clinger defensively.

"How much pay do you draw when you're behind bars?" asked Layne, tilting his head and looking directly into the outlaw leader's eyes.

Clinger flared a match with his thumbnail, cupped his hands around the flame, and lit the cigarillo. The evening breeze whipped away the smoke as he said, "Same old Layne Britton. Too pure to run with the likes of Cole Clinger.''

"Purity has nothing to do with it," Layne said blandly. "We want different things out of life, Cole. Since each man has to live his own, you go your way, and I'll go mine.''

"Fair enough," responded Clinger. "Your business gonna keep you in Wichita for long?"

"Maybe. You headquartering here?"

"For the time being.''

One of the riders spoke up, "Yeah, Britton. Cole's sweet on a Wichita woman. Till he finally gets the message that she ain't sweet on him, we'll be hanging around here!''

Clinger eyed the man narrowly and growled, "You shut up, Jones.''

Layne Britton was eager to be moving toward the Kellogg place. With a half smile, he said, "Nice to see you, Cole. I've got to be going.''

Clinger smiled in return. "Offer still stands, Layne. Maybe we'll run into each other in town. If you change your mind—"

"Not a chance," Layne cut in.

Shrugging his shoulders, the outlaw leader let smoke trail from his nostrils and said, "Well, at least you can let me buy you a drink in town. Or are you too pure to drink liquor bought with outlaw money?''

Without a word, the tall man gave Clinger a hollow look and nudged his horse westward. Irritated at the loss of time, he put the mare into a gallop.

Clinger and his men rode slowly toward town. As he rode, Clinger tried to think of a way to convince Layne to join with him and his band of gunmen—he needed Layne's expertise. Clinger had promised one of his accomplices, Charlie Prior, that he would break him out of the Fort Dodge prison. And he wouldn't leave Kansas until he freed the man and won the hand of Nelda Monroe.

Facing the setting sun with the wind in his face, Layne Britton gave the horse her head. Letting his own body find the rhythm of the animal's, he moved speedily toward Uncle Cyrus's ranch.

The sun cast lengthening shadows across the fields of waving grass, dotted with towering cottonwoods, elms, and rough-barked oaks. Birds nestled in the trees and flitted about the fields where cattle grazed lazily. This was a relatively flat world—the eye could see to where its green edges dropped off into an endless blue void. Wild flowers of myriad colors made spectacular points of beauty against the dark soil.

Alone with his thoughts, Layne Britton battled the doubts that were constantly following him. He relived the events of the day.

Was there nowhere in this savage land where he could lose himself? Where he could settle down and be at peace? Maybe he should go back east, where there were no fame-hungry gunfighters. He was sick of gun smoke, sick of bloody saloon floors, sick of stepping over dead bodies lying on dusty, sun-bleached streets.

Layne's steel-gray eyes swept the prairie around him, catching the motion of the tall grass as vagrant winds played across the endless fields. He took in the broad expanse of earth from horizon to horizon. The tall, handsome man shook his head. There was no way he could live in some crowded eastern city. This raw, untrammeled, wide-open country was in his blood. *Might as well crawl into a coffin right now and let them nail the lid shut if I have to leave this country,* he told himself.

He knew there was only one solution to his dilemma: settle down somewhere in the West, tough it out, and make the best of it.

As he slowed the bay to a trot, Layne told himself his best opportunity was right here. Uncle Cyrus had laid fifteen hundred acres in his lap. Ozzie Gisler had said it was the biggest single ranch in the Wichita area. If the Kellogg place was as rich in grass as what he had seen thus far, he could make a good living here.

Up ahead, Layne saw a shapeless cluster of buildings. Soon he drew nearer, and the ranch buildings took form as he approached the gate. He was pleased that the fence seemed to be in good repair. The house and barn were settled deep in a stand of cottonwoods, with various out-buildings scattered about. The barn was fringed on three sides by a large, rail-fence corral. A lazy stream wound its way across the property, providing nourishment for the trees that lined its banks. Layne realized it could also provide irrigation for the pastures and hay fields.

Riding the half mile from the gate to the house, Layne dismounted, making a mental note that the buildings would need fresh paint. He crossed the big yard, doing a quick survey of the outbuildings and barn. He found some doors sagging on loose hinges and saw that a couple of roofs needed repair.

Layne glanced westward as he walked toward the long, low-roofed house. The horizon was growing heavy with lavender as the golden rays of the late sun shafted upward through broken, low-hanging clouds.

The floorboards of the porch creaked under his weight as he crossed to the door. It was unlocked, and the hinges complained of the intrusion as he entered the large kitchen. Everything seemed intact, as it must have been the day Uncle Cyrus died, except for a heavy layer of dust. Slowly, he moved from room to room. The furniture was in good condition in all but one bedroom, where a windowpane was broken, allowing rain and snow to blow in.

Returning to the kitchen, he found a candle and matches in a cupboard. Lighting a candle, he stood it in a tall glass and set it on the big table. Weary from the long, hard day, he dusted off a straight-backed chair and eased into it. As flickering shadows danced on the walls, he assured himself that with a few days' work the place could be made presentable and livable.

Layne looked around the kitchen and thought of Cyrus Kellogg. The old man had lived alone for a long time. Aunt Sadie, his wife, had died in her late forties. Layne told himself that the house really needed a woman's touch. As that fact pressed itself home, haunting, familiar thoughts scratched at his mind . . . thoughts he had crowded far back into his subconscious for years: *A man needs a woman*.

But what decent woman would have a gunfighter? This had been Layne's burden for years. Men who lived by the gun could have their share of cheap-perfumed, heavily painted women, but the wholesome kind, with whom one built a home and raised children, remained unattainable.

Layne felt the darkness bearing down as the old feeling of despair began to wash over him. Stubbornly, he shook it off, determined to start his life unencumbered with the past. No matter what happened, Layne Britton was going to settle down right here and build a cattle ranch. He would throw himself into it with all that was in him. Given enough time, his name would fade from people's memory. When young gun hawks no longer hunted down and challenged Layne, he would look for a woman with whom he could share his life and raise a family.

The tall man stood up, blew out the candle, and moved outside. A full moon was rising in the east. Leisurely he strolled past the barn and circled the corral. Looking across the broad fields, he eyed the stream, which reflected the orange of the moon. Somewhere among the dark, looming trees an owl hooted. The crickets were giving their nightly concert. Layne took in the night sounds and smells until the moon had detached itself from the horizon and transformed into a silver disc.

The bay mare nickered softly as Layne emerged from the shadows and mounted her. Horse and rider moved up the dusty path and passed through the gate. As Layne viewed the bright, moonlit road before him, an even brighter beam of hope seemed to light his path. His lifelong dream just might be coming true.

Connie Lee awoke to the early morning sun beaming through the windows. Her mind felt dull and her body was still tired. Having lain awake till nearly dawn, she had slept only two or three hours. She wondered what had awakened her. Then from downstairs came tinkling and clattering sounds from the kitchen. Dolph Catron was apparently attempting to prepare his own breakfast, something he had never done.

Rolling out of bed, Connie walked to the dresser and picked up a hairbrush. While she ran the brush through her long dark locks, she thought of her visit from Ozzie Gisler. The dear old man had come the evening before to offer his sympathy. As they had sat on the porch, Connie had desperately wanted to tell him of the conversation with her dying mother. Uncle Ozzie was the only person to whom she could bare her heart. But Connie had refrained. She wanted to verify some things before telling Ozzie of the burden she was carrying.

Tying up her hair in a blue-green ribbon that almost matched her eyes, the lovely woman donned a robe and descended the stairs. As she entered the kitchen, Dolph Catron was bent over the stove, muttering swear words to himself. As she asked what he was doing, he turned his bulky frame around to face her.

Catron was in his mid-fifties. He had thinning gray hair on a broad head, with a flat face. Beneath his heavy gray mustache was a thick-lipped, down-turned mouth. He had cold black eyes and a fixed, feral expression on his face. Even when he smiled, which was seldom, he bore a savage look.

Catron was not smiling when he said to Connie, "Trying to light a fire so I can have some breakfast." The dark suspenders that held up his gray pants stood out in contrast to his white undershirt, which was open to the chest, exposing wiry gray hair.

Moving closer, Connie said, "You go shave, Dolph. I'll fix your breakfast."

Catron showed his surprise. "I didn't think you'd ever do it again."

"As long as I live in your house, I'll cook your meals," she said, lighting the fire, her manner congenial but distant.

A half hour later, Dolph Catron reappeared, groomed and dressed. The kitchen smelled of hot food. Wordlessly, he sat down at the table. Connie laid the food before him and took her place at the opposite end, with only a cup of coffee.

Catron eyed her with speculation and asked, "Aren't you going to eat?"

"I'm not hungry," she replied levelly.

Connie sipped at the coffee while her stepfather wolfed down his breakfast. After several minutes, he said around a mouthful of scrambled eggs, "You planning on moving out of this house?"

"Yes."

"How soon?"

"Quick as I can make arrangements."

"What do you have in mind?"

"I think Nelda Monroe will let me move in with her. I can pay my way as soon as I get a job."

"Job?"

"Mr. Weneke told me not long ago that I could work in his store when Mother was gone."

Dolph Catron's broad brow furrowed. "Working in the general store is all right, Connie, but I don't want you living with Nelda. You know what she is."

"*Used* to be," Connie insisted.

"Well, she'd still be a bad influence on you."

"Nelda is a fine woman, Dolph. She's altogether different from what she was when she worked the dance halls. She lives as decent a life as any of the respectable women in Wichita. She's in church every Sunday. That's more than can be said for you."

Catron's face darkened. "Well, she's going to be getting married to Gisler pretty soon, isn't she? Then what'll you do?"

"That's all her idea," commented Connie. "It's doubtful that she'll ever corner Uncle Ozzie."

"Why don't you just stay right here?" asked Catron, lifting his dark gaze to the young woman's face. "You're welcome to."

Malice glimmered in Connie's emerald eyes, making it all too clear how she felt about him.

Catron laid down the fork in his hand, wiped his mouth with a napkin, and said gruffly, "All right, let's hear it. What did your mother tell you?"

"The truth!" snapped Connie.

Pulling out a big cigar, Catron said, "And that is . . . ?"

"That you were carrying on an affair with my mother!" she lashed. "An affair that resulted in my father's leaving, and our home being broken by a divorce!"

Catron bit the end off his cigar. "Your mother was in love with me," he said casually. "What's the matter with that?"

Connie's eyes narrowed, and her face turned red as she said in a low, controlled voice, "She was in love with your money!"

The stout-bodied man placidly lit his cigar and puffed on it heavily. "That's your opinion."

"That's what she told me on her deathbed!" Connie fought her tears, not wanting to give Catron the satisfaction of seeing her so upset by him.

Remaining calm, his face smug, Catron asked, "What else did she say?"

Connie stood up, fighting to control her emotions. "Mother confessed that she had lied about how my father felt about me. Both of you lived a lie. You let me despise my father for something he had never done!"

Catron swore, his face twisting wickedly. "What do you mean?" he bellowed. "Morgan Lee left this town and never showed you one ounce of concern."

Connie's eyes flashed with anger. "That's a lie! He left me a letter, and Mother burned it!"

Complacently, Catron shrugged and looked at the burning tip of his cigar. "Okay, but if he cared anything for you, he'd have tried to contact you again."

Fury rioted in Connie's breast. "He did, Dolph Catron," she said heatedly. "And you intercepted all his letters and telegrams! You even stole the money he sent me for stage fare!"

"Your mother was delirious," he growled. "I never did any such thing."

Connie's mind was invaded by a fiery rage. Ignoring his defense, she said, "Do you realize what you caused me to do to my father? Have you thought of what my letter must have done to him?" Her voice was breaking. Tears brimmed her angry eyes. "What kind of a beast are you? How could you let me do such a thing when you knew my father was innocent?"

Dolph Catron's lips curved farther downward. "I told you Cora was delirious," he said coldly. "I never intercepted any letters or telegrams. I certainly never stole any of your money."

Connie could see through her stepfather to what he really was: a greedy, heartless, self-centered liar. She suddenly knew it was best she back off. He was liable to cover his tracks, and then she could never prove his vile deeds. It would be best if he was left off guard. "Since Mother isn't here," she said, feigning calmness, "I guess I will have to leave it at that."

"I tell you, she was delirious," Dolph repeated.

Without further comment, Connie began gathering dishes. Dolph moved to the kitchen door, stood watching the woman for a moment, then left the house. Only then did Connie allow her tears to flow.

Later that morning, Connie left the huge house and walked toward the business district. As she passed people on the street, they paused to express their sympathy at the death of her mother. Accepting their kindness with a smile, she moved steadily toward the telegraph office.

Reaching the office door, Connie stopped to speak to an elderly woman, then entered the small room. Ed Trask, the operator, was receiving a message. He looked up at Connie and smiled. Pointing toward a chair with his chin, he continued to write to the sound of the syncopated clicking. Connie eased onto the chair and folded her hands.

As the clicking stopped, Trask turned toward her and said, "Good morning, Miss Connie. Do you wish to send a telegram?"

"No, Ed," she told the elderly man. "I need to talk to you."

"Oh," he said, looking a bit puzzled. "What can I do for you?"

Connie held his gaze steadily and said, "Do you remember back when my parents divorced and my father left Wichita?"

"Sure. What about it?"

"In the months that followed, were there any telegrams that came for me from my father?"

Trask's eyes pulled away from Connie's gaze. He cleared his throat and shifted on the chair. "Well, uh . . . that's been a while. I—"

"Please, Ed," Connie said, entreating him earnestly. "It is very important that I know."

Trask ran a palm over his face. "Well, I was told that your pa had mistreated you, and that even though the telegraph messages sounded as if he loved you, they really were designed to upset you. So . . . so . . ."

"*Who* told you that?" cut in Connie.

"Well . . ." Trask cleared his throat. "Well, Miss Connie, it was Dolph Catron."

"And you gave all the telegrams to him?"

"Yes'm," Trask answered nervously.

Standing up, Connie smiled broadly and patted his hand. "Thank you, Ed. You have been a real help." Quickly, she turned and passed through the door.

The Wells Fargo office was right next door. Entering, she saw the agent, Harry Dunn, sitting at his desk.

"Hello, good-looking," the forty-year-old Dunn said with a warm smile.

"Hello, Harry," she said, returning the smile.

"Sorry I couldn't attend your mama's funeral yesterday," said Dunn, "but I had the Dodge City stage coming in, and I couldn't leave the office."

"I understand."

"Were you looking for Uncle Ozzie?"

"No," replied Connie. "I wanted to talk to *you*."

"Well," grinned Harry, "wait'll old Ozzie hears about this! He thinks he's the only man in town you care about."

Connie smiled lightly and said, "Harry, do you remember the letters from my father that came for me for several months after he left Wichita?"

Dunn dipped his chin. "Well . . . uh . . ."

"I know about the letters, Harry," said Connie. "There's only one thing I want to know."

"Connie," Dunn said timorously, "I don't want—"

"Dolph and I have already discussed this," she said with persistence. "I just want you to clear up something for me. Harry, it's very important."

Dunn rubbed his chin.

"What reason did Dolph give you for intercepting my letters?" she asked, pressing him.

Still rubbing his chin, Dunn said, "Well, Connie, he told me that Morgan Lee had abused you, and the letters were only filled with further abuse. To protect you, he asked me to channel all the letters to him. Dolph really loves you, Connie."

"Sure," she said hollowly. "Thank you so much."

Connie left the Wells Fargo office, her face set in lines of despair. Her mother's dying testimony was true. Dolph Catron had encouraged Cora to deceive her, and together they had painted a black, warped picture of Morgan Lee. As Connie headed down the boardwalk, she felt the stinging pang of guilt again. The bitter words of her letter to Morgan Lee ran through her brain, over and over.

Suddenly, she was aware of a familiar voice calling her name from across the street. It was Nelda Monroe.

Connie stopped and waited. Nelda paused, allowing a wagon loaded with children to pass, then proceeded toward her young friend.

Connie Lee looked at Nelda fondly as she drew near. Now approaching fifty, Nelda rued her fading beauty but still kept herself quite presentable, dressing her full-bosomed figure so as to maintain her femininity. She had big brown eyes and wore her auburn hair in an upsweep. Though she still caught the eyes of many men, her sole objective was to win the heart of Wichita's foremost stagecoach driver.

"Connie!" said Nelda excitedly. "Wait till you hear!"

Looking into the woman's dancing eyes, Connie said, "It must have to do with Uncle Ozzie."

"Yes!" exclaimed Nelda. "I just left his house. And you know what? He told me that if he was going to be in town Saturday night, he would take me to the barn dance!"

Connie Lee knew Ozzie Gisler. He was on the run from Nelda and planned to keep on running. Even so, he did like Nelda's attention, though he would not admit it, and often said things to keep her on the string.

Smiling, Connie said, "Mmm-hmm. The old rascal must have said that because he knows he'll be gone."

"I know," chuckled the older woman. "But it's a step in the right direction. Now that he's said it once, he'll say it again. One of these times he is going to slip up and forget which day he's pulling out for Dodge City. I'll unleash my womanly powers on him, and he'll never want to stop dancing with me!"

"Well, good luck," said Connie, patting her friend's shoulder.

For a few moments, the two women discussed Connie's situation, and it was decided that she would move in with Nelda as soon as she started to work at the general store.

Connie considered telling Nelda Monroe what she had learned from her dying mother, but she decided to wait. She wanted to talk to Ozzie Gisler about it first. Nelda did not seem eager to move on, so to make conversation, Connie asked, "Nelda, have you heard anything from Robert?"

Nelda's face sagged, and sadness filled her eyes as she thought of her son, who was serving twenty years at the Fort Dodge prison for his role in a bank robbery. Shaking her head, she said, "No. It's been four months since he's sent a letter. I guess old Mom doesn't matter when you're twenty-six years old and in prison."

Touching Nelda's arm, Connie spoke tenderly, "I'm sure you matter to Robert. There probably just isn't anything for him to write about. I mean, every day must be pretty much the same in prison."

"I know, honey," said Nelda wistfully, "but he could at least write and let me know he is all right."

"Maybe you just need to get on Uncle Ozzie's stage and go to Fort Dodge," Connie said. "I'm sure they would let you into the prison to see Robert."

She nodded and said, "I'm going to send another letter, and if Robert doesn't answer, I think I'll do just that." Nelda's face suddenly pinched. "Oh, Connie," she breathed tremulously, "do you suppose Ozzie doesn't want to marry me because of Robert? Maybe he doesn't want to bear the shame of having a stepson who is in prison."

"No, I'm sure that's not it. The old scalawag has just been a bachelor too long. He's afraid of losing his freedom."

Nelda managed a smile. "I hope that's all it is. If he only realized that I would not tie him down. I would just work hard at making him happy."

Connie patted Nelda's arm again. "You just stay after him," she said encouragingly. Turning to leave, she added, "I'm on my way to see him right now. I'll put in a good word for you."

Nelda thanked her friend and watched her walk away. Wheeling and heading up the boardwalk, Nelda saw a lone rider angling his horse toward her. The instant she saw his face, she looked away and walked more quickly.

Cole Clinger goaded his horse and intercepted her at the corner of Becker's Pharmacy. Nelda stopped, taking hold of the partially finished railing that was attached to the building. One side of it had the sharp points of several nails exposed.

Using his horse to block Nelda from stepping onto the street, Clinger said, "Hello, darling."

The woman's eyes flashed fire. "I'm not your darling," she said stiffly.

Dismounting, the outlaw moved close to her, saying, "Nelda, I don't know why you fight it. You know you're attracted to me."

"Like I'm attracted to a polecat," she retorted disdainfully.

Moving closer, Clinger said, "You're just playing hard to get."

"I've told you before, Cole Clinger. I want nothing to do with you or anybody like you."

Nelda started to walk away, but the repulsive outlaw stepped in front of her. Nelda stopped, eyeing him with contempt. People passing nearby watched the scene.

"Look, honey," said the hatchet-faced man, "you and I were meant for each other."

Nelda raked his face with her burning eyes. "Quit dreaming, Cole!" she snapped. "You and I have nothing in common."

"What about your outlaw son?"

"I can't help what Robert is."

"Nelda, honey," said Clinger, waggling his head, "don't tell me we're not alike. I know what you used to be."

A haze of anger clouded the woman's eyes. "You said it right, buster! *Used* to be! I'm not proud of what I was, and I'm trying to live it down." Looking around at people passing by, she added, "Being seen with the likes of you isn't helping any. Now, you get away from me, Cole Clinger. And stay away!"

The outlaw felt a prickle of anger run over his scalp. As he started to take Nelda in hand, his eye caught a movement to his left side. Checking himself, Clinger looked to see the imposing form of Marshal Roy Templeton flanked by his deputy, Tom Olson.

Wichita's town marshal was a thick-bodied man in his early sixties. He had a firm jaw and a look in his eyes to match. Templeton was tough and tolerated no nonsense. He had survived fistfights and gunfights with the best that outlawry could produce.

"This man giving you trouble, Mrs. Monroe?" asked the marshal huskily.

"Nothing that I can't handle, Marshal," said Nelda, eyeing Clinger up and down with contempt.

Fixing the outlaw with a hard look, Templeton said levelly, "Cole, I told you that I'd leave you alone as long as you behaved yourself in my town. I know what you are, but I've got nothing on you in my jurisdiction." Squinting his eyes, he added with a hiss in his voice, "But you get out of line just once, mister, and I'm gonna drop you in a deep hole and tell God you died."

Raising his hands palms forward, Clinger said, "I wasn't meaning to cause no trouble, Marshal. You certainly can't jail a man for talking to a nice-looking woman."

"It's all right, Marshal Templeton," Nelda spoke up. "Mr. Clinger was just about to get on his horse and ride away. But thank you for your concern."

The husky lawman tipped his hat to the woman, gave Clinger an appraising look, and walked away. The young, lanky deputy followed.

Nelda looked up at the outlaw and said, "You *were* about to mount your horse and ride, weren't you, Clinger?"

Keeping his voice low, the outlaw said, "I'm only hanging around this town because of you."

"Then you can move on!" came Nelda's tart reply.

Clinger took a quick look down the boardwalk. The two lawmen had disappeared. He seized Nelda, pulling her close. She caught the foul odor of his breath just before his lips pressed her own. Struggling against him, she made a gagging sound deep in her throat. When Clinger released her, she slapped his face savagely.

The repulsive outlaw was stunned by the blow and thrown off balance. He stumbled against the tacked-up railing, gashing an arm on the exposed tip of a nail. He reeled and fell into the dusty street at the feet of his horse. Wordlessly, Nelda pivoted and walked away.

Cole Clinger eyed the blood spurting from the stinging gash in his arm and shouted, "You come back here,
Nelda! Come back!" He started to curse.

Nelda smiled to herself as she moved away. Cole
Clinger was using words that even she had never heard.

Chapter Five

Leaving Nelda after their conversation on the boardwalk, Connie made her way toward Ozzie's place. As she turned the corner of First Street, she was suddenly aware of a towering figure moving in her direction. He wore a light-gray Stetson that matched his expensive, western-cut suit.

When Connie's eyes lifted to the man's angular face, she was taken with his rugged good looks. His skin was well tanned, and his dark, neatly trimmed mustache contrasted with his even white teeth when he smiled and touched his hat brim. A strange sensation swept over Connie as she found her voice, released a smile, and said, "Good morning." She wondered who the handsome stranger was as she bid her fluttering heart to return to normal.

The tall man paused, looked into her eyes with his steel-gray gaze, searched momentarily for his own voice, and returned Connie's greeting. Layne fought the urge to turn around and take another look as Connie passed him. Swallowing his heart, he gave in, stopped, and wheeled. With the leisure to observe, he saw again the full black mourning dress that emphasized her narrow waist and stunning figure. Her movements were graceful and poised, and she walked with her back arrow straight.

As Layne Britton watched her move away, he knew this had to be Connie Lee. Although she fit Ozzie's description, this young woman was much more. Her facial features remained as vivid in his mind as if he were still

56

looking at them. Her heart-shaped face was exquisitely
framed with hair as black as midnight. He knew he would
not easily forget her large emerald eyes or her perfectly
formed nose above full, ruby lips.

Layne smiled to himself as the lovely creature disappeared beyond the next corner. Shaking his head, he thought,
*If that is not Connie Lee, my eyes couldn't take the real
thing!*

As Connie walked to Waco Street, she decided there
was only one thing to do. She must go to Fort Dodge and
see the man who had been so ill-treated by her mother, her
stepfather, and herself.

Abruptly, fear gripped Connie. What if Morgan Lee
would not want to see her? Words from her scathing letter
came back to her. *Be sure you understand this. I mean it. I
never ever want to see you again.* Fighting tears, Connie
said aloud, "Oh, Daddy . . . you've got to see me. I must
explain that I wrote the letter under a false impression. I
was only fourteen then. I was sick at heart and deeply
hurt. Please, I'm your only daughter. I—"

Suddenly the wave of cold fear claimed her again. *My
father may have remarried!* Maybe he had other children.
Maybe there was another daughter who was responding to
his love. Connie clenched her hands into fists. *Daddy may
have totally crossed me out of his life!* Wiping tears from
her eyes, Connie told herself that in spite of these dark
possibilities, she must try to reconcile with her father.

Connie turned north onto Waco Street. She could see
Ozzie Gisler in front of his little house. He was on top of
the bright red Concord stagecoach, scrubbing it down.
Moving slowly toward him, Connie knew what she would
do. She would write a letter to Morgan Lee explaining
Cora's deathbed confession. She would ask his forgiveness
and request his permission to come by stagecoach to see
him.

Connie would ask Ozzie Gisler to carry her letter
personally to Morgan Lee, since Fort Dodge was not far
from Dodge City. If her father rejected her, the trip to
Fort Dodge would be unnecessary. She prayed that this
would not happen.

When Connie was within fifty yards of the spot where Ozzie Gisler was scrubbing vigorously on the Wells Fargo coach, a tiny ball of iron-gray fur bounded toward her, yipping gleefully. Puddles jumped into Connie Lee's arms, licking her face as it wagged its tail affectionately. Connie held the little dog tight, stroking it tenderly.

The Concord coach glistened in the sunlight as soapy water ran down its sides. Brushes, lye soap, and water buckets were scattered around. From the top of the stagecoach, the wiry Ozzie grinned from ear to ear and said, "Hello, beautiful!"

"Hello, handsome!" came Connie's reply.

Scrambling down to the ground, Ozzie asked, "Do I have to drive all the way to Dodge to get another hug and kiss?"

"Maybe," she said, a sly look in her eyes.

"Well, I'll tell you this much," he cackled. "It'd be worth it!"

Connie hugged Ozzie's neck with her free arm and planted a kiss on his scraggly cheek. "You need to sharpen your razor," she said playfully.

Ozzie guffawed. "I have to leave my face bristly like this in order to fight off all the women!"

"Well, I'll just remember that," said Connie.

"I didn't mean the whiskers are there to fight *you* off, honey. A woman that *really* loves a fellow will smooch him in spite of the whiskers. In fact, a *real* woman enjoys it."

"Oh, is that so?"

"Sure is."

"Does Nelda enjoy it?" Connie asked with a gleam in her eye.

Ozzie's leathered face crimsoned. "Now look here, sprout," he said, "me and Nelda have never been that close together."

"I'll bet!" teased the lovely woman.

"It's the blessed truth!" insisted Ozzie. "The only she-male in this here world that gets the privilege of kissin' Ozzie Gisler besides you is Puddles!"

Connie held the little ball of fur close to her face and

said, "Well, please be assured that Puddles and I realize the great blessing that you have bestowed upon us. But really, Uncle Ozzie, we would be glad to share you with Nelda."

The old man shook his head and said, "You didn't walk all the way over here to nudge me about Nelda. Did you have something more important to discuss?"

"I believe your relationship with Nelda is very important. I understand you're taking her to the barn dance Saturday night."

"No, honey," said Ozzie, "I'll be on my run to Dodge City."

"But Nelda told me you said—"

"What I said was, if I wasn't on my run to Dodge, then I'd take her to the dance."

"That's what I came over here about." Connie struggled to keep a straight face.

"What's that?" asked Ozzie, eyeing her suspiciously.

"I was just at the Wells Fargo office. Harry Dunn said he received a telegram from the office in Dodge City. They want you there for something special next Wednesday, so you won't be pulling out till Monday. Isn't that wonderful? You'll be here Saturday night!"

Connie's insides were about to burst as she watched the old man's windburned face transform to a pasty white.

Eyes enlarged, he said, "You been eatin' too much chicken without fryin' it?"

"It's the truth, Uncle Ozzie," she said in dead seriousness. "Harry specifically asked me to come over and tell you. As soon as I leave, I'll go by Nelda's and let her know. I think it's just great! Since you wanted to take Nelda to the dance so bad, now you can do it!"

Ozzie Gisler looked sick as he staggered to the porch of the house and eased into an old chair. Connie followed, about to explode.

"What's wrong?" she asked innocently. "You *are* glad for the news, aren't you? This will give you and Nelda a chance to get really close. And just think! The moon will be full, so you can walk her home in the moonlight. The honeysuckle will be strong on the night air. Who knows what will happen?''

Ozzie swallowed hard, staring blankly. He felt like a trapped animal.

''Just think, Uncle Ozzie, it won't be long until I can call her *Aunt* Nelda!''

Ozzie wiped a nervous hand over his sweat-beaded brow. ''C-Connie,'' he gasped, looking at her as she stood over him, holding Puddles. ''You . . . you gotta help me. I can't go through with this.''

''What's the matter, Uncle Ozzie, dear?'' she said in a singsong manner. ''Didn't you really mean it when you told Nelda you would take her to the dance if you were going to be in town?''

Still staring blankly, he said, ''Well, I . . . uh . . .''

Connie could hold back no longer. Bursting into laughter, she covered her mouth with her hand.

Ozzie looked up, blinking. Slowly he realized that the woman had pulled one over on him. His color came back, and a smile of relief crept over his face. ''You fibbed to your Uncle Ozzie. You had me believin' that I really was gonna have to—'' Suddenly, he joined Connie in her laughter.

When the laughing had subsided, the old stage driver wiped his brow again and said, ''You really had me scared, Connie. I could almost hear the weddin' bells.''

''Uncle Ozzie,'' smiled Connie, ''being married to Nelda would be good for you. It would put so much more meaning into your life.''

''Nonsense!'' he breathed. ''With some woman fixin' up the house and hangin' curtains and puttin' down rugs, a fellow would have to ask permission to spit!'' They both laughed, and then Ozzie's expression grew serious and he asked Connie why she had really come to see him.

The merriment in Connie's lovely eyes drained away as she sat down on the porch step and released Puddles. Feeling the woman's distress, the old man sat down beside her. ''What is it, honey?'' he asked tenderly.

With effort, Connie began. She told Ozzie of her mother's deathbed confession, and the old man shook his head as he heard of Dolph Catron's part in the deceit. Tears spilled as Connie shared the guilt that burdened her.

"Oh, Uncle Ozzie," she sobbed, "I've got to see my father. I must tell him how sorry I am. He's got to know how I feel . . . and that I love him."

Putting an arm around her shoulders, Ozzie said, "Well, honey, we'll just see to it that you get to see your daddy. What can your old Uncle Ozzie do?"

"The first thing I'm going to do," said Connie, sniffling, "is write him a letter and explain it all. Then I will tell him how sorry I am and how very much I love him."

"Mmm-hmm," he hummed. "That's the thing to do."

"How far is the fort from Dodge City, Uncle Ozzie?"

"About five miles."

"Would you do me a big favor?"

"You name it, darlin'."

"If I give you the letter before you pull out in the morning, would you take it with you?"

"Of course," grinned the old man.

"Would you have time while you're in Dodge City to take it personally to Daddy at the fort?"

"Sure, honey," Ozzie said assuringly. "I'll borrow a horse and ride out there with your letter. It'll be good to see your dad again." Shaking his head, he added, "I sure am glad to know he isn't the bad guy we were all thinkin' he was!"

"Yes," she replied, smiling through her tears. Looking at him directly, she said, "What if Daddy won't let me see him? What if he doesn't want me in his life again? What if—?"

Squeezing her tightly, Ozzie spoke consolingly. "Now, Connie, don't you fret your pretty head about a thing like that. Your father will welcome you with wide-open arms and a happy heart. I'm sure he'll be dyin' to see you."

"I hope you're right," said Connie. "But don't wait for Daddy's answer. I want him to have time to digest the letter. If he is willing for me to come see him, he will wire me."

"Whatever you say, Connie."

Drying her tears, Connie said, "I'll bring you the letter in the morning. You leave at seven, don't you?"

"Yes, honey. I won't pull out till that letter is in my hand!"

As Layne Britton continued down the boardwalk after meeting Connie Lee, he quickly relived their encounter. Her emerald eyes had been troubled and her lovely brow knitted. When her gaze had lifted to his, he had broken into a smile and reached for his hat brim. She had instantly returned a warm, friendly smile and said a simple, "Good morning." Layne remembered how his heart had slammed against his ribs, momentarily robbing him of his breath. Never had a woman's charms so captivated him.

The ex-gunfighter strolled toward Dolph Catron's office. Just ahead of him, a familiar figure stepped out of a small shop and grinned.

Bill Henderson, arm in a sling, said, "Howdy, Mr. Britton."

"How are you feeling, Bill?" Layne asked enthusiastically.

"A little weak in the left pinion," replied the amiable shotgunner. "Doc Wilson says I'll have to extend my vacation a couple of weeks. Personally, I think I could climb back in the box in less than a week. But he's the doctor."

Layne smiled. "Well, I'm glad you're better. But again, I really am sorry you got shot on account of me."

"Like I said, Mr. Britton, it wasn't your fault." Frowning slightly, Bill cocked his head and said, "Ozzie tells me you took out Pete Foss like you were drawing against a clay statue."

Layne let a crooked grin form on his lips. "Ozzie tends to stretch things a little," he said modestly.

Bill stepped a little closer and lowered his voice. "Mr. Britton, word is all over town that you're here."

"I was afraid of that."

"I think I should warn you."

"About what?"

"Boone Foss is spreading word that he's out to avenge his brother's death. He's supposed to be pretty fast. Talk is that he's going to challenge you."

The tall man went cold all over. He breathed an oath and said, "Will this thing ever end?"

"Just thought I'd warn you," Bill said, adjusting his sling.

"Appreciate it. Just take care of yourself."

"You do the same," said Bill.

Layne crossed the street, angling toward Dolph Catron's place of business. Entering the spacious office, he was greeted by a slender man in his mid-thirties.

"Good morning, sir," said the man, with a friendly smile.

"I would like to see Dolph Catron."

"Mr. Catron is not in the office at the moment. I am his assistant—Len Cummings. May I be of service to you?"

"I really need to see your boss," Layne said with a smile. "When will he be in?"

"Not before two o'clock," said Cummings. "He is looking at some land several miles out of town."

"Fine. I'll come back around two, then."

Layne Britton left the office and headed up the street to Weneke's General Store, which was the largest business establishment in Wichita. Layne stepped inside and made his way around several customers chatting and looking at goods. He saw a short, stocky, gray-haired man wearing an apron with the store's name on it and assumed him to be Herman Weneke. Making his way past shelves containing foodstuffs, cracker bins, and jars of hard candy, Layne found the clothing section. Two women were standing nearby. One of them whispered loud enough for him to hear, "That's him!"

Twenty minutes later, Layne left the store bearing a large package under one arm. He had purchased work boots, jeans, plaid work shirts, gloves, and a straw hat. Weneke assured him that he could supply tools, paint, fencing, and anything else that would be needed.

Towering, broad-shouldered Layne Britton held the attention of townspeople as he strode down the street toward the hotel. Two dance-hall women met him on his way. They looked at each other and then gave him wide smiles. Grinning back at them, he touched his hat brim and kept moving.

As Layne approached a vacant lot between two buildings, he saw a boy about nine or ten years old come around the corner of the nearest building. The lad was running from another boy and looking back with a stick in his hand that he was using as a gun. He shouted, "Bang! Bang! I'm Layne Britton, and you're dead!"

"Oh, no, I'm not!" shouted back his pursuer. "I'm Boone Foss. Bang! Bang! *You're* dead!"

The first boy, still looking back as he ran down the boardwalk, collided with Layne Britton. Quickly, Layne grasped him with his free hand to keep him from falling. The second boy skidded to a halt, looking up at the tall man.

Bending over, Layne said, "Whoa! Better slow down, there, boy. What's your name?"

"I'm Layne Britton!" the boy said excitedly, waving his toy gun.

"And I'm Boone Foss!" exclaimed the other one. "And I'm gonna kill Layne Britton!"

"No, I mean what's your real name?" asked Layne.

"Jimmy Eastland," responded the one who had collided with Layne.

Quickly the other one spoke up, "I'm Mike Spencer."

"Jimmy," said the ex-gunfighter, "why are you pretending to be Layne Britton?"

"Because he's the fastest gunfighter in the whole world! And he's here in Wichita right now. He's gonna square off with Boone Foss and kill him deader than a skunk!"

"Oh, yeah?" interjected young Mike. "Boone is faster than lightning! He's gonna shoot Layne Britton down like a mangy dog!"

"Boys," said Layne, "there isn't going to be any gunfight between Boone Foss and Layne Britton."

"How do you know that, mister?" asked Jimmy.

"Do you know what Layne Britton looks like?" Layne asked the boy.

"Sure do," responded Jimmy. "My pa told me. He seen him yesterday."

"Describe him for me."

"Well, he's . . . he's real tall, like you. And . . . and he wears a big gray hat, and a gray suit with black trim, and—" Suddenly, the boy's mouth sagged. His eyes widened.

Mike Spencer stammered, eyes bulging, "I . . . I r-really d-didn't mean what I s-said, Mr. Britton. B-Boone Foss isn't really gonna k-kill you."

"You're right, son," Layne said evenly. "Because there isn't going to be any gunfight." Looking at both boys, he added, "Gunfighters are fools. Do you hear me?"

"Yes, sir," nodded both boys.

"Now, go on and play. But forget this Foss-Britton stuff."

Layne left the youngsters standing on the boardwalk. He decided that since he had time before Dolph Catron's return, he would visit Ozzie Gisler. He had grown to like the bristly old-timer.

Layne Britton stopped briefly at his hotel and left the package of new work clothes in his room. As he reached the bottom of the stairs on the way out, he was approached by Chester Higgins. A tall, skinny man with tousled black hair stood behind him.

"Mr. Britton," said Higgins, smiling widely, "do you mind if my friend here takes a picture of Boone Foss's body with you standing over it?"

Layne eyed Higgins blankly.

"I'm Dewey Blankenship," spoke up the skinny man. "Just getting my photography business started here in Wichita. I know you wouldn't want any powder flashes while you and Foss are squaring off, but after the gunfight is over, it would boost my business if I could hang up a picture of you standing over Foss's body."

Layne gave both men a hard, impatient look. "Gentlemen," he said with sand in his voice, "there isn't going to be any gunfight." Spreading his coat, he added, "There can't be a gunfight without guns. You will notice that I have none. I am no longer a gunfighter. I am a cattle rancher. If you see Boone Foss, pass him the word."

"That's not the way Boone Foss tells it," said Higgins.

Layne's jaw squared. "Boone should tell the whole story," he said stiffly. "I was forced into that gunfight after his brother Pete shot Bill Henderson. They had five men holding guns on the passengers. Threatened to shoot them down if I didn't face him. I had no choice."

"Somebody needs to shut Foss up," put in Blankenship. "He's got men in this town trembling in their boots. Somebody needs to put him in his place."

"They will," Layne said dryly. "They always do."

He left the two men in the lobby and walked out to the street. Inquiring of a passerby how to find Waco Street, he headed toward Ozzie's. He had gone only a few steps when a big, ample-bellied man moved out of a doorway and blocked the path, the star on his vest flashing in the sun. There was a stern look on the marshal's face.

"Morning, Marshal," Layne said cordially.

Thumbs hooked in his bulging belt, the stocky lawman said, "I aim to make Wichita a peaceful place for decent folks to live."

"I'm all for you, Marshal," Layne said, smiling.

"I don't want any gunplay in the streets."

"I'm for that, too."

Squinting, Marshal Templeton asked, "You *are* Layne Britton, aren't you?"

"Yes, sir."

"What are you doing in Wichita?"

"I'm here on business."

"What's this I hear about you planning a shoot-out with Boone Foss?"

"You shouldn't listen to gossip," Layne said coldly. "I'm not planning a shoot-out. I killed his brother in self-defense. And to defend the people on that stagecoach."

Disbelief framed the lawman's bulky face. Through

clenched teeth, he said, "I don't like gunslicks in my town."

Layne was getting his fill of Marshal Roy Templeton. With a cutting edge to his voice, he said, "Then why don't you run Boone Foss out?"

"Can't till he breaks the law," Templeton said gruffly. "You, either. But if you—"

"I'm not a gunfighter anymore," Layne insisted, opening his coat to show he had no holster. "Hung up my gun."

Squinting again and looking narrowly into Layne's steel-gray eyes, the marshal said, "You on the level?"

"Yep."

"Then I'll ask it again. What's your business in Wichita?"

"I inherited some land southwest of town. Going into the cattle business."

"You really giving up slapping leather?"

"Really."

"Well, I'm mighty glad to hear it, son," said Templeton, relief on his features. "Nothing good ever comes from gun hawks hanging around."

"Reckon you're right, Marshal. All I ever saw when I packed an iron was trouble and death. I'm through with it."

"How'd this talk ever get started that you and Boone were going to shoot it out?"

Lifting his shoulders, Layne said, "Don't know. Maybe you ought to ask Boone."

"I'll do it," nodded Templeton. "Just make sure you stay clean."

"Plan on it," said Layne, nodding.

Templeton's bulbous face hardened. "I'm counting on that," he said, turning away abruptly.

Layne Britton continued on his way to Ozzie's house, shaking off his conversation with Marshal Templeton. When he spied the Wells Fargo coach as he turned onto Waco Street, he hastened his pace.

Drawing near the Concord, Layne observed the brushes and water buckets. A few more steps revealed the old stage driver sitting on the porch of his little house, talking to the captivating brunette Layne had seen earlier.

Both of them looked up when Puddles began to bark. Layne clapped his hands together, saying, "Here, Puddles!"

The little gray dog leaped off the porch as Connie and Ozzie got to their feet. With Puddles in hand, Layne entered the small yard.

"Howdy, son!" said Ozzie.

Layne flashed a smile at the old man, saying "Howdy" in return. But his helpless eyes were on the woman. His heart thumped his rib cage.

Connie smiled, taken again with a strange, unnamed sensation.

"Son, I want you to meet the prettiest woman in all the world," said Ozzie. "This is Connie Lee. Connie, this is Layne Britton."

Connie maintained the smile, extending her hand. Layne took it gently and said, "I'm pleased to meet you, Miss Connie. I believe we passed on the street earlier this morning."

"Yes, we did," she said. "I'm glad to meet you."

Releasing Connie's hand, Layne said, "Ozzie, she's everything you said, and more."

"Ain't she somethin'? I told you she'd pop your peepers!"

Connie's face tinted. "Oh, Uncle Ozzie."

"Let me express my sympathy, Miss Connie," said Layne softly. "I'm sorry about your loss."

"Thank you," Connie murmured.

"Layne's gonna become a permanent resident of these here parts," spoke up Ozzie.

"Oh, really?" Connie was pleased with the news. The tall man's good looks and masculinity left her breathless.

"Yep," continued the bristly old man. "He inherited the Cyrus Kellogg ranch. Old Cy was his uncle. Layne just found out the ranch was his a few weeks ago."

"May I say welcome, Mr. Britton?" said Connie. "I hope you will like our town."

Layne struggled against his pounding heart. "If the

rest of the citizens are as gracious as you, how could I help but like it?''

Connie blushed again.

"Come to think of it," Layne continued, "I have business with your stepfather this afternoon. He is handling the legal work on the inheritance.''

Connie Lee masked the repugnance she felt at the mention of Dolph Catron. Ozzie wanted to turn and spit, but checked the impulse.

"That's nice," said Connie. Taking a deep breath and letting it out, she embraced Ozzie briefly, saying, "Thank you for listening to me, Uncle Ozzie. I'll have the letter to you before it's time to pull out in the morning.''

"Okay, honey," he grinned. "See you then.''

Connie turned and presented the tall man with a warm smile. "It was a pleasure to meet you, Mr. Britton," she said sweetly. "Your name has a familiar ring to it. I'm sure I've heard it before, though I can't say where or when.''

Layne felt a chill travel up his spine as he returned her smile.

Connie bid them good-bye, walked to the gate, and started up the street. Ozzie had to call his dog back, who was bent on following her.

Forgetting that the old driver was there, Layne watched Connie till she passed from view. Even then his line of sight remained on the last spot where he had seen her. After a brief moment, Ozzie Gisler loudly cleared his throat. Layne pulled his gaze around to the weathered face.

"Better pull in your tongue, son," chortled Ozzie. "You're liable to trip on it.''

Layne's face reddened. Disconcerted, he shrugged his wide shoulders and said, "What are you talking about?''

"What am I talkin' about? Who do you think you're kiddin'? That female has got you so captivated, you don't even know what day it is!''

Layne laughed, saying, "I think you'd better get back to cleaning that stagecoach. It's got soap streaks all over it.''

"Well, if you're so observant, sonny, why don't you just pitch in and get to cleanin'?"

Layne pointed to his suit and said, "Sorry, Ozzie. I didn't come prepared for hard work."

"No wonder you had such trouble pullin' in your tongue!" Ozzie exclaimed, and both men laughed.

The two men teased and insulted each other while Layne stood by and watched Ozzie finish scrubbing the bright red stagecoach. At two o'clock, Layne left Ozzie's place and walked back to North Main, entering the Catron office at two-twelve. Len Cummings looked up from his desk with a friendly grin.

"Is Mr. Catron in now?" queried Layne.

"He sure is, sir," replied Cummings, rising. "Just have a seat, and I'll tell him you're here."

Layne dropped onto a chair as the slender man disappeared through a door into an inner office.

Inside the office, Cummings approached Dolph Catron's desk. Excitedly, he said, "Mr. Catron, he's here."

Looking up through a cloud of cigar smoke, the thick-bodied man said, "Who's here?"

"The man I told you about, sir. You know! The one who's dressed in a very expensive suit and just smells of money."

"Oh!" said Catron, a greedy smile capturing his thick lips. "Well, show him in, Len. Show him in!"

Layne looked up as Cummings emerged from the inner office. "Mr. Catron will see you now, sir," he said, gesturing toward the door.

Dolph Catron was on his feet behind his desk as Layne entered. A wide smile dominated his entire face. Reaching across the desk, he said, "I'm Dolph Catron. What can I do for you?"

Layne gripped the man's meaty hand, saying, "My name is Layne Britton."

The wide smile faded as Dolph Catron's features turned ashen gray.

Chapter Six

Layne Britton's words hit Dolph Catron with the force of a Kansas tornado. The appearance of Cyrus Kellogg's heir at this time meant that the fifteen-hundred-acre ranch would elude Catron's covetous grasp.

The avaricious attorney had been buying up land in and around Wichita as fast as he could in order to multiply his wealth and increase his political power. He was already chairman of the town council. When Wichita's growth would demand the establishment of a mayor's office, Dolph was going to be the town's mayor . . . no matter who had to be stepped on.

Much of Dolph Catron's land grabbing was done by crooked dealing. He had secretly hired two henchmen, W.D. Hunt and Big Jack McQuaid, to convince landowners to leave the area. Departing under fear of bodily harm, the frightened people sold their land cheaply to these two, unaware that Catron was behind the threats. Marshal Templeton was never contacted by the bullied landowners because Catron's men had warned that they would kill wives and children if the law was brought in.

Since the Cyrus Kellogg legal papers were in his office, Catron was fully aware of the time provision in the will. He had his eyes on the Kellogg ranch and was counting the days eagerly. Catron had already arranged to wrangle the ranch purchase dirt cheap and make the fifteen hundred acres his own. But now his plans were threatened.

71

Realizing the smile had deserted his face at the sound of the name Layne Britton, Catron recovered his composure and adopted a facade. *Thirty-nine days to go,* he thought. *Why did Layne Britton have to show up now?*

Speaking past his gray, swirling thoughts, the bulky man said, "Layne Britton? The gunfighter?"

"Ex-gunfighter," corrected Layne. "I've hung up my gun."

"Seems I've heard that's close to impossible for a gunfighter to do," said Catron, gnawing nervously on the cigar between his teeth.

"I'm giving it my best shot," said Layne. "No pun intended."

The thick-bodied attorney managed a chuckle and then gestured toward a chair at the corner of his desk. "Sit down, Mr. . . ah . . . Britton. Sit down."

Layne lowered his muscular frame onto the chair as Catron eased into his own. Trying to evade direct contact with Layne's steel-gray eyes, he said, "What can I do for you?"

"I understand that you took over your father's practice at his death."

"Uh . . . yes."

"You are probably aware of a will left to your father's care by the late Cyrus Kellogg."

"Oh, yes. I . . . I'm familiar with it," said Catron, still not meeting Layne's gaze.

"Then you know that I am heir to his ranch."

Catron's thoughts were in a jumble. Somehow he had to keep Layne Britton from laying claim to the ranch. "Well . . . uh . . . there's a time limit in the will, Britton," he said, thrusting an authoritative tone into his deep voice. "You're . . . ah . . . you're too late." Catron knew he was taking a chance, but he was desperate. Maybe Layne Britton would be dull enough to be blinded by his smoke screen. "The time limit ran out August twenty-eighth."

The crooked man's hopes were dashed instantly. Layne slid his fingers to an inside coat pocket. Producing a white envelope, he said, "You must be mistaken, Mr. Catron.

These papers my aunt gave me have the deadline as October twenty-eighth."

Dolph Catron's face colored slightly. "Oh, really?" Chewing uneasily on his cigar, he accepted the unfolded sheets from Layne Britton. Scanning the contents, he recognized his father's handwriting. A letter, along with a copy of the will, had been sent to Cyrus Kellogg's sister in Scott City. "Hmm," said Catron. "I could've sworn—" Looking past Layne, he hollered toward the door, "Len! I need you in here!"

Presently, the slender form of Len Cummings appeared. "Yes, Mr. Catron?"

Catron switched the cigar from one side of his mouth to the other with his ample lips. "Bring me the file on the Cyrus Kellogg estate."

Cummings nodded and disappeared.

Almost looking into Layne's eyes, the lawyer said, "Maybe there was an error in the copying."

Layne Britton found it difficult to trust a man who would not look him square in the eye.

Len Cummings returned. Catron opened the folder, read the point of concern in the will, and feigned surprise. "Well, what do you know? Reads the same here, Mr. Britton. My mistake. I sure would have bet my neck on August."

Layne thought of asking why, if the date had been August twenty-eighth, the ranch had not been put up for sale by now. But he let it pass.

"Sure am sorry about that," lied Dolph Catron, pulling the soggy cigar from his mouth.

"We all make mistakes," replied Layne flatly. Leaning forward, he said, "I'd like to lay claim to the place."

"Uh . . . yes, of course," responded Catron, clearing his throat. There had to be a way to salvage this unfortunate situation. But Layne Britton was no fool, and he would have to be stalled until it could be thought through. "It'll take a couple days to draw up the papers. You know . . . title deed in your name. That sort of thing."

"Sure," said Layne, standing up. "Since this is Friday, I'll give you till Monday afternoon."

"Fine," said Catron, also standing. Sweat beaded his brow as Layne Britton left the office.

The ex-gunfighter returned to the hotel and changed into his work clothes. After renting a wagon and team from the hostler, he drove to Weneke's General Store. There he bought cleaning supplies, paint, and brushes. Then he loaded the wagon and headed out of town.

As Layne Britton drove past the Broken Spur Saloon, Boone Foss sat on a bench in the shade and eyed him malevolently. When the wagon had rolled from view, the straw-haired boy sitting next to the gunfighter said, "When you gonna brace him, Boone?"

Swinging his cold gaze to Danny Smith's young, eager face, he replied, "When the time's right, kid. I'm gonna pick my own time."

"You really think you're ready for him?" asked Danny.

Boone's expressionless face leveled on the youth. "What's the matter, kid? You ain't got faith in your teacher? I'm showing you the tricks of the trade, aren't I? You've seen me whip this gun out, haven't you?"

"Yeah, Boone. But . . ."

"But what?"

"You saw him kill your brother. Pete was fast. Layne Britton must be a lot faster."

Boone snickered, tossing his head. "Compared to me, my brother was like Arctic molasses. You just stick with me, kid. I'll show you I'm faster than Britton. And what's more, I'll mold you into a real gunfighter. That *is* what you want, isn't it?"

Danny's lips trembled slightly. "S-sure, Boone," he answered, nodding. "Sure."

Eyeing the yellow-haired boy with speculation, Boone said, "Danny, you've lost some of your salt since you heard my brother took Layne Britton's bullet. Have you changed your mind about being number-two gun hawk in the whole world?"

Ejecting a timorous breath, Danny replied, "No. No,

sir, Boone. I . . . I just ain't sure I could ever be as fast as
Layne Britton.''

"Huh!'' Boone guffawed. ''He ain't so hot. I'll show
you. After I drop him, maybe you'll have enough confidence in me to know that I can train you till you make
Britton's draw look like a slow freight train!''

"Sure, Boone,'' grinned Danny.

"Well, let's drink to it, kid.''

"What?'' Danny said, incredulously.

"C'mon. It's time you had a drink.''

While Wichita's lamplighter moved from post to post,
illuminating Douglas Avenue, Layne Britton, returning
from his ranch, walked from the livery stable to the Sunflower Hotel. He ordered hot water and a large galvanized
tub brought to his room. They were delivered by Danny
Smith. As the boy poured steaming water into the tub, he
introduced himself, telling of the death of his parents and
of the subsequent offer of the hotel's owner to let him
work for his keep. When the youth departed, Layne eased
into the tub and leaned back, relaxing after the dusty ride.

At the same moment, Dolph Catron met with his two
henchmen in a windowless room behind Catron's office.
W. D. Hunt and Big Jack McQuaid sat on straight-backed
chairs facing Catron, whose face was etched with deep
concern. Slowly and methodically, he explained the situation of the Kellogg will. Layne Britton was a threat to
Dolph Catron's long-range plans. He must be eliminated.

"I'm thinking an ambush would be the ticket,'' Catron
finally said. "Catch him while he's coming or going from
the ranch.''

Big Jack McQuaid, who resembled a huge bulldog,
leaned forward. "Before we risk murder, boss, why don't
we give Boone Foss a crack at Britton?''

"What do you mean?'' asked Dolph.

"Word is out that Foss is itching to take on Britton in
a shoot-out to avenge his brother's death. You offer him
some money, boss, and you'll soon be rid of Britton.''

"If he's looking to brace Britton,'' Catron said quickly,
"why should I put out money?''

"Foss is taking his time—waiting for the right moment. A little cash on the barrelhead would hurry things up."

Dolph Catron pondered the suggestion for a moment. Then he shook his head, saying, "I don't know, boys. Layne Britton is fast. I doubt seriously Foss can take him."

"What have you got to lose, boss?" Hunt put in. "If Britton should kill Foss, we can go ahead and ambush him. But I'm with Jack. The less dirt on our own hands, the better."

"Guess you're right," agreed Catron. "I won't pay Foss anything till it's over. If Britton blows him away, I've lost nothing." Looking at McQuaid, he said, "You know where Boone Foss is?"

"Yeah. He's at the Broken Spur, bragging his mouth off about what he's going to do to Britton."

"Go get him. I want to talk to him right now."

Layne Britton finished his bath, dressed, and then ate supper at the Redwing Cafe. He had just returned to his hotel room when there came a knock on the door. Swinging it open, he looked down at Danny Smith.

Smiling at the boy, Layne said, "I dumped the water out myself, Danny. Buckets and washtub are ready—"

"That's not what I came for, Mr. Britton," Danny cut in. "I'm here to deliver a message."

"A message?"

"Yes, sir. A man is waiting for you down on the street. He says to tell you to strap on your gun and come face him."

Layne's blood turned cold. He knew who it was, but he asked the question anyway. "What's his name?"

"Boone Foss."

"You tell this Boone Foss I don't jump at anybody's command," Layne said evenly. "You can also tell him he knows I don't even own a gun. But if he wants to see me, he can come up here."

"Yes, sir, Mr. Britton," said Danny, backing away. "I'll tell him."

Leaving the tall man standing in the door, Danny

wheeled, rounded the bannister, and darted down the stairs. Passing through the lobby, he hurried outside. Boone Foss and Dolph Catron's two henchmen were waiting across the street. It was a warm night, and many of Wichita's citizens were milling about.

"He ain't coming down, Boone," said Danny, drawing near.

Boone's face stiffened. "What do you mean, he ain't coming down?" he demanded.

"Mr. Britton said to tell you that he don't jump at nobody's command," replied the boy. "He said he don't even own a gun, but if you want to see him, you can come up there."

Boone Foss swore. "Same thing he pulled on my brother," he said, disgusted.

"I don't believe he don't have a gun," said Big Jack McQuaid emphatically. "It ain't natural."

"He's got a gun, all right, and I aim to make him buckle it on," Boone Foss said.

"No sense wasting time, Boone," put in W. D. Hunt. "If you want that five hundred Dolph offered you, just go on up there to Britton's room and challenge him."

"Oh, no," snapped Boone. "When I gun down Layne Britton, it's gonna be right here on the street where all these people can see it! When I become king, I want lots of folks to attend the coronation!" Rubbing his chin, he added, "Enough folks are up and moving around early. I'll be right here in the morning when Mr. Layne Britton comes out that lobby door. You boys'll be with me."

"Sure will," agreed Hunt. "If he ain't wearing a gun, he can borrow mine."

Boone Foss grinned maliciously and said, "Not that it'll do him any good."

Chapter Seven

Connie Lee prepared herself a light meal that evening in the high-ceilinged kitchen of the big Catron house. As was often the case, Dolph had not come home after office hours, so she dismissed him from her mind. While she ate, visions of Layne Britton floated through her mind. She was puzzled by the strange, nameless feeling that had come over her both times she had seen the man. *What is it about him?* she asked herself.

Connie knew she was overwhelmed by Layne's towering form, his striking good looks, and his conspicuous masculinity. But there was more. She sensed a strange resolve within him, yet he was possessed of a kind and gentle spirit. Never had a man like this crossed her path before.

Connie spoke Layne's name audibly and then repeated it several times. There definitely was a familiar ring to it. Where had she heard that name before?

Finishing her meal, Connie slowly washed and dried the few dishes, as if hoping to put off the momentous task that lay before her. She must write a letter to her father.

Leaving a lamp burning low in the entrance near the front door, Connie climbed the stairs and entered her room. With the door closed, she moved to the dresser, struck a match, and touched the flame to a ready wick. The kerosene lantern brought the furnishings to life with a soft glow. Moving methodically across the large room,

78

Connie lit another lamp and set it on her rolltop desk. Taking out a piece of blank paper, she sat down and lifted a pen. Before dipping it in the inkwell, she let her thoughts drift back over the years.

Sweet memories of childhood embraced Morgan Lee's daughter. She could see the smiling faces of her parents and feel once again the contentment a child knows in a happy home that is filled with love. Connie remembered old dreams she used to have of someday having a marriage like that of her parents.

Precious times spent with her father came back vividly. She could feel again the deep satisfaction of knowing that he loved her dearly—the strong sense of security she once found in her father's presence. Then, abruptly, the stained memory of that crushing day when she came home to learn of her father's departure washed over her like ice water.

Holding the pen in hand and staring at the blank paper, Connie thought of how she had tried to hate her father. She recollected the day she found a photograph of Morgan Lee in her room and wrote "I hate this man" across his face. Then she had thrown herself on the bed, clutching the picture and sobbing uncontrollably. The tortured girl could never quite allow her pain and bitterness to force her to the point of actually hating Morgan Lee. Somehow the love Connie had once felt for her father always lurked beneath the surface of her emotions.

Through a mist of tears and struggling with her shaking hand, the heavy-hearted woman began to write. After two lines she stopped, laid down the pen, and crumpled the sheet of paper. Crossing the room, Connie went to the dresser. Pulling a handkerchief from the top drawer, she wiped her tears and blew her nose.

Back at the desk, Morgan Lee's daughter took a fresh sheet and started again. Rewording the letter, she wrote nearly half a page, paused, read it over, and wadded it up. The proper words were difficult to find.

Rising from the desk, she began pacing the floor. She would form the letter in her mind first. Little by little the words began to fall in place. Periodically she went to the desk and jotted some notes.

At one point while Connie walked the floor, she heard Dolph Catron's heavy footsteps ascending the stairs. Noticing the light under her door as he moved down the hall, Catron paused and called, "Connie!"

"Yes?" she responded.

"Are you still up? It's late. You ought to be asleep."

Connie felt bitter anger leap within her. What did Dolph Catron care about her well-being? He certainly had not hesitated to destroy the relationship she had had with her father. Suppressing the desire to tell Catron it was none of his business, she forced a pleasant tone and said, "I'll be going to bed shortly."

"All right," came Catron's deep voice. "Good night."

Connie did not answer. She waited until he moved down the hall and closed his bedroom door. Resuming her slow walk, she continued the mental composition of the letter. It must not be too long, yet it had to convey what was in her heart.

It was after two o'clock when she signed the words, *Your loving daughter, Connie.* Carefully, she read over the page-and-a-half letter. Satisfied that it made proper explanation of the lies she had been fed by Dolph and Cora and that it appropriately described her love and her desire to see him, she folded it neatly and slipped it into the envelope. Tears were flowing again as she sealed the envelope and addressed it.

A few moments later, Connie snuffed the lanterns and crawled into bed. Before dropping into a sound slumber, she whispered, "Please, God. Help him to forgive me."

Layne Britton rolled out of his bed in the near dark. Donning his work clothes, he left the room, anxious to get in a full day's work on the ranch house. As he crossed the lobby, Fred Yates, the sleepy-eyed clerk, was just moving behind the desk.

"Morning," Layne said.

"Good morning, Mr. Britton," yawned the clerk. "What you doing up so early?"

"Lots of work to do," Layne said over his shoulder as he passed through the door.

The sun had begun to flush the eastern sky as Layne pulled away from the livery stable in a rented wagon. Soon Wichita passed from view as he headed west on Kellogg Road.

Back in town, three figures sauntered down Douglas Avenue and stationed themselves on the boardwalk across the street from the Sunflower Hotel. Big Jack McQuaid and W. D. Hunt sat down on the edge of the walk and began rolling smokes. Facing the hotel, Boone Foss leaned against the hitch rail, a burning cigarette dangling from the center of his lips.

W. D. Hunt flared a match. "If he comes out this early, Boone, you ain't gonna have much of an audience."

"Just don't want to miss him," replied the cold-eyed young gunman. "I'll think of a way to delay the shoot-out after I challenge him."

The three men waited, talked, and smoked while the sun floated skyward and brightened the town. Wagons and buggies began to stir dust as they passed, and people were starting to mill about on the street. Several people had come out of the Sunflower, but there had been no sign of Layne Britton.

Growing impatient, Big Jack McQuaid lifted his huge frame from the edge of the boardwalk. "Maybe one of us needs to go over there and flush him out."

Boone Foss looked up into his broad and blunt face and said, "We tried that last night, remember?"

"Maybe I used the wrong word," grunted the immense man. "One of us needs to go over there and *drag* him out."

"You volunteering?" Hunt asked.

Adjusting his hat, McQuaid said, "Be right back."

There was no one in the lobby as McQuaid shouldered his bulky frame through the door. The big man climbed the stairs after checking Layne Britton's room number in the register. With the ball of his fist, he hammered loudly on the door. When there was no response, he banged harder. Suddenly the door of the adjoining room burst open. A man in his long johns stepped out, scowling at McQuaid. He swore and growled, "Hey, you! Cut out that racket! You trying to raise the dead?"

McQuaid took three strides and unleashed a vicious blow to the man's jaw. He went down hard and lay still, out cold.

McQuaid was wheeling to crash the door of Layne Britton's room when Fred Yates came bounding up the stairs two at a time. "What's going on up here?" he demanded, reaching the top. Suddenly he spotted the unconscious man sprawled on the hall floor and halted in his tracks. Swinging his gaze to the tall, hulking figure of McQuaid, he said, "Did you hit this man?"

"Naw," replied McQuaid, wagging his big, ponderous head. "He came charging out that door and accidentally ran right into my fist."

The skinny clerk took in McQuaid's size and said calmly, "Weren't you knocking on his door?"

"Nope," McQuaid said huskily. "I was knocking on number seven."

"If you're looking for Mr. Britton, he isn't here. He left before sunup."

"Where'd he go?"

"I have no idea," said Yates. "He said something about having a lot of work to do."

Without comment, the huge man left Yates standing over the man on the floor and noisily descended the stairs. Stepping into the brilliant sunlight, he crossed the street and said, "He ain't in his room, Boone. The desk clerk said he left before sunup. Said he had work to do."

"He's gone to the ranch," spoke up W. D. Hunt. "Probably be there all day."

"Well, let's go out and get him," said McQuaid.

"Just simmer down," Boone Foss said, waving an open hand at the big man. "He'll be coming back late in the day. We'll be right here waiting for him. C'mon. Let's get some breakfast."

As they headed for the nearest cafe, the shiny red Concord stagecoach rounded the corner of First Street and North Main. With Puddles on the seat beside him, Ozzie Gisler guided the prancing team up the street. He did a full

turn and drew the vehicle to a halt in front of the Wells
Fargo office.

Harry Dunn stood on the boardwalk conversing with
passengers. Ozzie set the brake and, smiling broadly, said,
"Mornin', Harry."

"Morning, Ozzie," grinned the agent.

As the old driver was climbing down, Puddles suddenly began barking. She hopped from the seat to the roof
of the coach and ran to the rear edge. Wagging her tail,
which put her total rear end in motion, she barked excitely.

Ozzie turned to see the comely form of young Connie
Lee making her way down the street. Puddles darted from
side to side, wanting to jump off the coach. The old driver
reached up and took her in his hands. Gently, he placed
her on the ground. The gray, yipping puff of fur bounded
up the street. Connie scooped the little dog into her arms.

Ozzie and Harry Dunn were packing luggage into the
rear boot when Connie approached the stage.

"Mornin', gorgeous!" Ozzie said in a chipper voice.
"Want to go with your old Uncle Ozzie? We got an empty
seat."

Smiling warmly, the lovely brunette said, "If this
letter does what it's intended to do, I'll be going with you
next time."

"I can guarantee it will," said Ozzie, encouragingly.
"There ain't no man on the face of this earth who could
resist you, honey. Leastwise your own daddy."

A slight tint brushed Connie's face. "Oh, Uncle
Ozzie," she said shyly.

"That's the blessed truth!" spoke up Harry Dunn.

The passengers were climbing aboard as Ozzie Gisler
took the letter from the woman's hand. "Now, don't you
worry over this here letter, darlin'," he said tenderly.
"Your old Uncle Ozzie will plant it personally in the hand
of Colonel Morgan Lee. If you were *my* daughter and I got
a sweet letter tellin' me you loved me and wanted to see
me, I'd fall all over myself gettin' a message to you!"

"I hope he feels the same way," Connie said anxiously.

"Not a question in my mind about that," the old man
said assuringly. "Now, let me have that pesky pup."

Ozzie lifted Puddles to the driver's seat and then turned and embraced Connie. As she planted a kiss on his leathery cheek, he said softly, "I'll see you in a week. This here letter *will* be delivered."

"Thank you," she said with a smile.

Ozzie turned to mount the coach as his substitute shotgunner was doing so on the other side. Suddenly, a female voice called, "Ozzie!"

Looking around, he saw Nelda Monroe hurrying toward him. She carried a brown paper bag in one hand. Ozzie's cheeks turned gray as a winter sky. Connie watched the scene with delight.

"H-hello, Nelda," he stammered.

"I brought you something," said Nelda sweetly, drawing near.

"Oh?"

"I made you some cinnamon rolls." She extended the paper bag.

Ozzie cleared his throat. "Why . . . uh . . . thank you, Miss Nelda. I sure do appreciate that."

As the slender stage driver accepted the bag, Nelda said, "You take care of yourself, do you hear?"

"Yes'm," nodded Ozzie, backing up. "I'll . . . I'll sure do that, ma'am."

Nelda winked at Connie and then, stepping to Ozzie quickly, pressed his scraggly cheeks between her palms and pecked him on the lips. "That's for good luck," she said, releasing him.

Swallowing hard, the flabbergasted stage driver said with difficulty, "Er . . . uh . . . thank you, ma'am." Quickly he spun and climbed up to the box. He kicked off the brake and yelled, "Hee-yah!" The four horses broke into a trot as the Concord rocked on its leather thoroughbraces and rolled away.

Hands on hips, Nelda Monroe laughed as the coach rounded the corner and disappeared. "Did you see his face, Connie? Old cute-stuff was hard pressed for words there for a minute!"

Connie laughed, too, and was joined by Harry Dunn.

Still laughing, Harry said, "You ever gonna ball-and-chain that ornery critter, Nelda?"

"Sure am," Nelda replied. "That old boy's days are numbered!"

The afternoon sun was dropping low as Layne Britton left his ranch and moved eastward on Kellogg Road. Work on the ranch house was coming along well. He had run out of paint in the early afternoon, so he had decided to check the fence all the way around the place. A few spots needed some minor repair. There were sufficient tools and wire in the supply shed, but no heavy staples for securing barbed wire to the fence posts. He had left a bit early so he could get to Weneke's store and pick up some before closing time.

As Layne left Kellogg Road and headed toward town, he noticed unusual activity around the big red barn on a farm owned by a man named Clarence Overman. A huge black and white banner on the side of the building announced the barn dance that would begin at eight o'clock that evening.

Moments later, Layne entered Wichita and proceeded to the general store. He parked the wagon out front and headed inside. Customers were thinning out as closing time drew near. The tall man made his way among the stacks of goods to the hardware area. As he searched for the fence staples, a familiar feminine voice caught his ear. It was Connie Lee.

Layne Britton's heart leaped within him. Moving toward the sound, he saw Connie standing by the grocery counter in conversation with another young woman about her same age.

Layne was totally unnoticed as Connie said excitedly, "Oh, that's wonderful, Betty Ann! I'll bet it won't be long until he pops the question."

Betty Ann's eyes were aglow. "A lot of things happen when there's music and a full moon," she giggled. Her mood turning suddenly serious, she said, "How about you, Connie? Are you going?"

Connie sighed wistfully. "No. I'm just going to spend a quiet evening at home."

Touching Connie's arm lightly, Betty Ann said, "Honey, you have been cooped up too long. We all admire you for taking care of your mother as you did, but she's gone now. You need to socialize. The most you've done for three years is attend church service when you felt it safe to leave your mother for that long. Why don't you come to the dance tonight?"

"Sounds like fun," agreed Connie. "It *has* been a whole three years since I've been to one." Shaking her head, she added, "But it's so soon after the . . . the funeral. And anyway, no one has asked me, and I'm certainly not going to go alone!"

"If the young men of Wichita knew you were open to invitation, there'd be a stampede to your door!" exclaimed Betty Ann.

Connie laughed dryly. "I doubt that! But maybe by the next barn dance, word will get around that I'm back in circulation."

"But honey," argued Betty Ann, "there'll be plenty of fellows there without dates. You wouldn't even sit out one dance."

"It's just not in me to do it like that," Connie said. "I just wouldn't go without an escort."

From behind Connie came a voice. "I'd be delighted to take you, if you'll go with me."

Both women turned to see Layne Britton moving closer. Betty Ann's eyes widened at the man's striking form. Connie's heart quickened.

Layne had surprised himself at giving in to a sudden impulse. It was not like him. He always carefully planned important moves, but the words were out before he knew it. There was something about this woman that flustered his normally calm, self-possessed manner.

Connie Lee's voice had deserted her.

Smiling broadly and removing his straw hat, Layne found himself saying, "Will you, Miss Connie? I would be deeply honored to be your escort for the evening."

"Connie!" breathed her friend. "Where have you been hiding him?"

The emerald-eyed woman reached deep and found her voice. "Oh . . . ah . . . Layne Britton, I would like you to meet Betty Ann Stewart."

Layne made a partial bow and said, "I'm pleased to meet you."

Betty Ann curtsied politely, saying, "Likewise, I'm sure."

Looking at the tall man, Connie said, "You know Bill Henderson. He's taking Betty Ann to the dance tonight."

Layne nodded, then turned to Betty Ann. "Is Bill up to dancing?"

"Well, no. We're just going to sit on the side, but at least we can be there." She turned to her friend and said, "I must be going, Connie. Will I see you at the dance?"

Connie's eyes flicked to those of Layne Britton. "Were you serious?"

"As a horse with a broken leg," he smiled.

With her heart thundering again, Connie said breathlessly to Betty Ann, "Looks like you'll see me there!"

Connie watched Betty Ann Stewart leave the store and then turned back to Layne. "I'd best be going," she said, smiling nervously. Inwardly she was reprimanding herself for being so unstable in this man's presence.

"I'll rent a surrey and pick you up about seven-forty," said Layne.

"Oh, no," replied the woman. "Everyone in town always walks to Overman's barn."

"Okay," agreed Layne. "What if I come by at seven-fifteen?"

"That will be just fine," she breathed. "Now I must be going."

"Just one thing," came Layne's resonant voice.

"Yes?"

"Where's your house?"

Connie's hand flew to her mouth. "Oh! I guess you would need to know that, wouldn't you?"

"It *would* save time," he grinned.

"Well, First Street is one block west of here."

"Yes."

"I live halfway down First Street toward Market Street. It's a large white house. You can't miss it."

"I'll be there." The handsome man smiled.

Connie floated out the front door, closing it behind her. Layne had started back to the hardware section when the door burst open. Connie's face was tinted as she hurried to the grocery counter. A sackful of groceries stood there alone. Grasping it, she smiled sheepishly at Layne and disappeared speedily.

Five minutes later, Layne emerged from the store carrying a box of staples. He climbed in the wagon and drove it to the livery stable.

The rim of the sun had just dipped below the western horizon as Layne strolled along Market Street and turned onto Douglas, noting the activity on the streets. As he headed toward the hotel, box of staples in hand, he was suddenly aware of three men moving toward him, blocking his way. Layne did not break his stride as the men fanned out and halted. As he drew near, he pulled up in front of the middle man, Boone Foss, who spread his legs and glared insolently at Layne. The malicious look in Boone's narrow-set eyes was unmistakable. Hair bristled on the back of Layne Britton's neck. A crowd began to form.

"Hello, Britton," Boone said. "Where's your gun?"

"Don't own one," Layne replied with gravel in his voice.

"You're a liar!" blustered the hawk-nosed man, pleased that the crowd of spectators was growing. "I'm challenging you, Britton! It's time you paid for killing my brother. I'll wait right here. You go to your hotel room and get your goddamn gun."

"I told you I don't own a gun. I'm not a gunfighter anymore."

Boone Foss's temper grew. "You can't do this!" he snarled, teeth bared. "You got to face me man to man . . . gun for gun! If you don't do it, you're yellow!"

From somewhere deep within, Layne Britton drew the

strength to curb his anger toward Boone Foss—his desire to dispose of this mad dog. Looking at him calmly, he said, "I'm through shedding blood, little man. Someone else will have to spill yours." Then Layne stepped around Boone and walked toward the hotel.

There was low talk among the crowd. Layne could hear Boone swearing vehemently at him as he passed into the lobby and mounted the stairs.

Chapter Eight

Promptly at seven-fifteen, Layne Britton knocked on the front door of the big white Catron house. He was dressed in his elegant gray suit and Stetson hat. When the door swung open, his heart seemed to fracture his ribs. Connie Lee was stunning in a green dress with a flared skirt and a form-fitting bodice trimmed with lace. A broad ribbon to match held her jet-black hair in an upsweep with bouncing ringlets in the back, and a beautiful cameo brooch graced her lovely neck.

Smiling despite her nervousness, Connie said, "Good evening, Mr. Britton."

"Mr. Britton was my father," Layne said with a smile. "My name is Layne."

A hint of crimson showed in Connie's lovely face as she dipped her chin and said, "Good evening, *Layne.*"

"May I say, Miss Connie, you look beautiful beyond words."

"Thank you," she responded. "But if I am to address you as Layne, you can drop the miss."

"All right, Connie," he grinned. "Now that we've dispensed with the formalities, may I escort you to the dance?"

"You may," she said, stepping onto the porch and pulling the door shut.

Connie and Layne fell in among the others who were making their way toward Clarence Overman's barn. Skulk-

ing in the shadows between two buildings, Boone Foss and
Dolph Catron's henchmen watched the couple go by.

The big barn was gaily decorated with bright-colored
lanterns strung overhead on thin cords. On an elevated
platform, four men were tuning up two guitars, a banjo,
and a fiddle.

Many of Connie's friends expressed their pleasure in
seeing her at the dance, admiring her tall, good-looking
escort. The young men eyed him with envy.

On the platform, the fiddler quieted the crowd. When
he had their attention, he said loudly, "All right, everybody!
It's time to get this shindig under way! So grab your
partners and here we go!"

He raked the bow across the strings and started his
foot tapping. The banjo led out, followed by the guitars.
The bow touched the strings again and the fiddle went into
a reel. Couples were swinging across the floor, while those
on the sidelines clapped their hands and stomped their feet
to the beat of the music.

Layne looked down at his partner. "Well, Connie,"
he said, "I'm afraid I'm pretty rusty."

"You couldn't be any rustier than I am," she chuckled,
taking his hand. "Let's go!"

The touch of Connie Lee's hand sent a tingle through
Layne's body. Instantly they were part of the swinging,
twirling, bouncing throng.

On the sideline, Bill Henderson and Betty Ann Stewart sat holding hands. Periodically, as Layne and Connie
swung by, Betty Ann would wave and smile.

Boone Foss stood in a partially shadowed corner,
leaning against the wall. His eyes followed Layne Britton
as the tall man glided his beautiful partner across the floor.
Boone could watch Layne only from a distance, however;
Marshal Templeton was attending the dance and had warned
that there would be no gunfighting. Templeton had his
eyes trained on Boone just as closely as Boone's eyes were
trained on Layne. It was quite obvious that as long as
Layne danced with Connie, he had no intention of fighting;
he was not wearing a gun, and his eyes never once strayed
from Connie's face.

During the third number, Connie noticed Nelda Monroe come in and sit down alone on a bench. When the song was finished, she suggested they take a break and led Layne by the hand to where Nelda sat.

When Nelda saw Connie approaching, she stood up and set her gaze on the tall, broad-shouldered man.

"Layne," said Connie, "I want you to meet my friend, Nelda Monroe. Nelda, this is Layne Britton."

The older woman's recognition of the name did not escape Connie's notice. As Nelda extended her hand, she said, "So you're Layne Britton?"

"You know of him?" asked Connie.

Something in Layne's eyes warned Nelda against saying too much. "Well . . . ah . . . yes," she said evasively. "I've heard about the attractive young man visiting Wichita who . . . ah . . . is staying at the Sunflower. So glad to meet you, Mr. Britton."

"The pleasure is mine . . . Miss . . . or is it Mrs.?"

"It's Miss Monroe at the moment," Nelda replied quickly. "Well, that is, it *was* Mrs., but—"

"What she means," cut in Connie, "is that she's working hard at making it Mrs. Ozzie Gisler!"

Layne's eyes lit up. "Well, what do you know! Ozzie didn't tell me about you!"

Nelda laughed, "Well, I'm Ozzie's little secret!"

Layne and Connie chatted briefly with Nelda and then excused themselves and walked to where Bill Henderson and Betty Ann Stewart were sitting. Joining them on the bench, they entered into light conversation.

Across the room, Danny Smith's dancing partner, a thirteen-year-old redhead, was taken up by another boy, and Danny wandered to the corner where Boone Foss leaned idly against the wall.

"Howdy, Boone," Danny said warmly.

"Who's the girl?" asked Boone.

Looking back at the dance floor, Danny replied, "Oh, that was Michelle Overman. Her dad's the one who owns this barn."

"You get in free?" chortled Boone.

Danny grinned sheepishly. "Sort of." Then in a seri-

ous tone he asked, "Hey, Boone, would it bother you to
talk about your brother's shoot-out with Layne Britton?"

Boone gave the boy a blunted look and then said
woodenly, "I guess not."

Eyes sparkling, Danny said, "I've heard tell that
Britton moves like a well-oiled machine. Is that right?"

"Yeah, you might say that."

"Word is that Pete never got his gun out of the
holster."

Boone Foss eyed young Danny Smith prudently. Finding the subject distasteful, he nodded and clipped his
words, "Pete was fast, Danny. He just wasn't in Layne
Britton's league."

"How'd Pete find out about Layne being on the
stagecoach?"

"Friend of ours in Dodge City saw him climb aboard
and sent a telegram."

On the dance floor, Layne and Connie whirled by,
smiling at each other.

Boone ran a hand over his mouth and said in an
envious tone, "Britton's not only fast with a gun, he's also
fast with the ladies. Every young buck in town has been
itchin' to make time with Connie Lee. He comes to Wichita a perfect stranger . . . and look at him!"

"She is right pretty," acknowledged Danny. Returning to his subject, he said, "What about you, Boone? You
still gonna challenge him?"

"Of course I am. It's only right that I do it for my
brother. You keep your eye on Britton, you hear, kid? Let
me know when he comes and goes from the hotel. He's
not going to get away from me. Got it, kid?"

"I got it, Boone. When we gonna practice shooting
again?"

"Maybe tomorrow," Boone said.

As Danny continued to talk to his hero, Layne Britton
surreptitiously watched the two. Moments later, Danny left
Boone and reclaimed Michelle Overman. After several
more numbers, the musicians took a fifteen-minute break.
The crowd gathered around the punch bowl, while some of

the young men headed outside with a jug. Boone Foss went with them.

Layne spotted Danny Smith standing alone. He left Connie with Betty Ann Stewart and Bill Henderson and walked to where Danny stood.

"Evening, Danny," Layne said with a smile.

"Hi." The boy smiled in return.

"Would you let me give you a little free advice, Danny?"

The boy eyed Layne with speculation. "I suppose."

"Son, you don't have any parents to guide you, so I'd just like to advise you to stay away from the likes of Boone Foss. He's bad medicine."

Danny stiffened. "Well, *you're* a gunfighter, too."

"I used to be," corrected Layne. "But I was never an outlaw. Foss runs with Cole Clinger. You know what they say about birds of a feather."

Danny dipped his head. "Yeah."

"I hate to see you mess up your life, son." He laid a hand on the boy's shoulder.

Danny smiled weakly and said, "I'll be more careful."

"Good," said Layne, squeezing the shoulder. "That's a right pretty girl you're dancing with."

"You ain't doing too bad yourself."

Layne ran a finger over his dark, neatly trimmed mustache. "Think so, huh?"

"Miss Connie is the prettiest woman in Kansas, that's for sure," said Danny.

Layne dismissed himself and returned to the spot where Connie was in conversation with Betty Ann, Bill, and two other couples.

As the music started again, the dance floor filled up quickly. Moments later, Nelda Monroe was sitting at her place on the bench when she saw a surly figure enter the barn. Her skin crawled as she recognized Cole Clinger. The hatchet-faced outlaw paused just inside the doorway, his dark eyes roaming the crowd. Nelda was about to turn her back when she saw Sid Gilbert, the town lush, totter up to Clinger. Gilbert stood in front of Clinger, talking earnestly to him. The outlaw was trying to ignore Gilbert as he continued searching the crowd.

Suddenly Clinger spotted Nelda. He brushed the stammering drunk aside and headed for the woman. Nelda felt her skin prickle again as the repugnant man drew near. She spied a bandage where the nail had cut his arm on their previous meeting.

Clinger halted, standing over Nelda. "Hello," he said, showing his tobacco-stained teeth.

Malice glimmered in Nelda's eyes as she said througl tight lips, "Crawl back under your rock, Clinger."

A sullen petulance darkened the skin around his eyes. "You got no call to talk to me like that," he growled. He pulled his lips into a smile. "I'll forgive you for gashing my arm if you'll dance with me."

With calculated indifference, Nelda said, "I don't want your forgiveness."

"Now look, woman," Clinger said, bending down to her, "I've had enough of you playing hard to get."

"When it comes to you, horse-breath, the word is *impossible*." Nelda's eyes flashed fire.

A haze of anger clouded Clinger's face. His voice matched his heated resentment. "Well, from what I seen, you been throwing yourself at that—" The outlaw was suddenly conscious that people were staring. Sitting down on the bench, he lowered his voice. "That Fargo driver ain't your kind, Nelda."

"Look, Clinger," she said, losing patience, "I had enough of your kind when I worked the saloons. John Monroe came along ten years ago, married me, and took me away from that life. He adopted my fatherless son and gave me something to live for. I found out what decent living is, and I like it. I'm through with your kind. Do you hear me?"

"John Monroe's dead, Nelda. He can't help you anymore. But Cole Clinger's alive. You want to get married? I'll marry you."

"I'm not marrying an outlaw!" she breathed hotly.

With a sneer, Clinger said, "Your *son* is an outlaw."

Nelda's eyes flashed again. "That doesn't mean I

approve of it! Robert became an outlaw because he ran with bad company. Scum like you!''

Ignoring her biting words, Cole Clinger stood up, gripped Nelda's shoulders, and pulled her to her feet. ''You're gonna dance with me right now!''

Arching herself away from the foul-smelling outlaw, Nelda wrenched from his grip and slapped him violently across the face. Clinger staggered from the blow, blinking his eyes. The music stopped, and the dancers followed suit. All eyes were on Clinger and Nelda as Layne Britton threaded his way through the crowd, Connie following.

Towering over Clinger, the formidable ex-gunfighter said, ''Cole, you'd best take yourself somewhere else. I think Miss Nelda has made herself clear.''

Cole Clinger showed obvious respect for Layne Britton. ''All I was doing, Layne,'' he said with an innocent tone, ''was asking for a dance.''

Connie Lee was taken with surprise that the two men were acquainted and on a first-name basis, but she showed no outward sign of it.

''You're not dancing with me,'' Nelda said icily.

Clinger looked at Nelda, slid his glance to the crowd, and then settled it on Layne. ''I'll still buy you that drink, Layne, when it's convenient,'' he said amiably.

As the outlaw turned to leave, he nearly collided with Marshal Templeton. Sidestepping the lawman, Clinger moved outside. He heard Templeton ask if there was a problem and Layne Britton assure him that it had been settled.

Suddenly, Clinger heard the shuffling feet of Sid Gilbert, the town drunk.

''Hey, Cole,'' slurred Gilbert, ''wait up!''

The outlaw turned to face him in the yellow light of the lanterns. The music resumed inside the barn.

''Listen, Cole,'' said the unsteady man. ''I'd . . . I'd be your own personal bodyguard if you'd just take . . . take me into your gang.''

''I told you before,'' said Clinger brusquely, ''I've got all the men I need right now.''

"But Cole," argued Gilbert, eyes drooped, "when I'm sober, I'm a mean devil with a gun. You really—"

"When I see you sober and I need another gun, I'll consider it," lied Clinger. With that, he turned and walked into the night.

Inside the barn, the musicians were playing a slow ballad, and the guitar player was singing.

Connie looked up into Layne's handsome features as they danced across the floor. She was fighting her runaway heart. What kind of man was this tall stranger? How did he know the infamous Cole Clinger? Why would Layne want to settle down at ranching if he had outlaw connections? Quickly, she erased that thought. There had to be some reasonable explanation for Layne knowing Clinger. This tall, gentle man was no outlaw. Ozzie Gisler liked him, and Ozzie was an expert judge of character.

Layne gazed into Connie's heart-shaped face. He was overwhelmed by her soft, emerald-green eyes and captivating features. Then and there he made up his mind he was going to see more of her. *One thing for sure,* Layne told himself, *I will tell her of my past before someone else does.* Suddenly it occurred to him that Connie had been standing right there when he had confronted Cole Clinger. Certainly she knew the outlaw's reputation.

Holding her gently, Layne said, "Connie, there are only a few dances left. I need to talk to you. Would you mind if we left now?"

"Of course not," she responded warmly.

The couple passed by Nelda Monroe and explained that they were leaving early. Nelda smiled her approval and told them that since Danny Smith's date lived right here, she was going to walk with him back to town.

The attractive couple passed from view, and Nelda turned her attention back to the music. A quarter-hour later, she waited for Danny to bid Michelle Overman good night at the farm house.

Leaving the porch, the gangly youth approached the woman and said, "Okay, Miss Nelda, we can head for town now."

As they walked among other moonlit figures, Danny asked, "You wanted to talk to me, ma'am?"

"Yes, Danny," she said, slipping her hand in the crook of his arm. "I hope you won't think I'm a nosy old biddy."

"I'd never think that, Miss Nelda," he said assuringly.

"Well, Danny," began Nelda, "you know I have a son who is in prison over at Fort Dodge."

"Yes, ma'am."

"Robert used to be a good boy. Like you, Danny."

Danny was silent.

"But he went bad when he was sixteen. Just two years older than you are right now."

Danny nodded. "What made him go bad, Miss Nelda?"

"He met a young outlaw," she responded. "This fellow was only twenty-one, but he was a hero to Robert. His name was Jess Kramer. Everything Jess did, Robert wanted to copy. I tried to talk sense to Robert, but he wouldn't listen. Jess Kramer could do no wrong."

"Somethin' bad happened, huh?"

"Yes," Nelda answered grimly. "Robert was with Jess and his gang when they held up a bank over in Dodge City. He was their lookout. He never even went inside. Shooting started inside, and a bank employee and two customers were killed. The townspeople rallied instantly. Robert and the others were captured."

Nelda swallowed hard and continued. "Jess Kramer and the others were hanged. The judge went lighter on Robert because he wasn't in on the shooting."

"How long did the judge give him?"

"Twenty years," she said, choking on the words.

Danny waited a moment, then said, "How come Robert is in the prison at Fort Dodge? Isn't that just a military prison?"

"It was during the Civil War," explained Nelda, "but since the war, so many outlaws run these parts that there aren't enough jails and prisons to hold them. So they use the facility at Fort Dodge for federal prisoners and men with long sentences."

"I see," nodded the boy.

"What I wanted to talk to you about, Danny, is your relationship with Boone Foss. I saw you talking to him in the barn."

Danny Smith was quiet for a long moment. Then he said softly, "I've already had one lecture on the subject tonight."

"Oh?"

"Yeah, by Layne Britton."

"He's been around," said Nelda, glad for Layne's concern for young Danny. "You'd best heed the lecture."

Lifting his eyes toward town, the youth averted the subject by saying, "Looks like they're going to leave the town all lit up till everybody gets home from the dance."

The silver moon cast their shadows on the road before them as Connie and Layne walked at a leisurely pace toward town. He liked the feel of the slender, graceful woman at his side, and the touch of her hand on his arm.

"Connie," Layne said nervously, "it might be well if I tell you a little about myself."

Lifting her eyes to his shadowed face, she said, "All right."

"You know Cole Clinger?"

"I'm sorry to say that I do."

"You could tell he and I have met before."

"Yes." Connie nodded, glad that her mind was about to be put at ease.

"I've never been an outlaw," Layne said hastily, "but I *was* a gunfighter. I met Clinger in St. Joseph. He wanted to hire my gun."

Stopping, Connie exclaimed, "That's it! I knew your name rang a bell. I just couldn't place it. I've heard people talk of your skill with a gun."

Looking into her eyes, he said, "Does it change your mind about me?"

"You said you *used* to be a gunfighter?"

"Yes."

"What you once were is not important, Layne," she said smoothly. "It's what you are *now* that counts."

"Well, I'm *almost* a cattle rancher," he chuckled, as they resumed walking. "As of Monday afternoon, I will be the legal owner of the Cyrus Kellogg ranch. Your stepfather is preparing the papers. All I have to do is finish fixing up the place and buy some cattle, and I'm in business."

"Is the ranch run down pretty bad?"

"Not really. Just some light repair work on the out-buildings and some fence mending. I've already done some cleaning and painting on the inside of the house."

Layne brought the subject back to himself, telling Connie of his past and bringing her up to the present. He told her of the incident with Pete Foss and of Boone Foss's challenge, issued that very day. He shared with Connie the nagging dread that other gun hawks would keep showing up.

Connie expressed her confidence that Layne Britton was a man of purpose and that in time he would live down his gunfighter image.

Connie and Layne were unaware of the eyes watching from the shadows as the couple moved up Market Street and then turned left on First Street. Leaving the light of Market's yellow lanterns, they strolled once again in pale moonlight and soon were in the yard of the big white house.

Connie paused at the steps of the porch and looked up at Layne, his angular profile outlined against the silver dimness of the night sky. Her heart tripped and fluttered. Struggling against the shortness of her breath, she said, "Layne, I'm glad you've hung up your gun. And I'm glad you're going to be settling on the Kellogg ranch."

Gazing intently at the moonlight in her eyes, he responded, "I really like Wichita."

For a brief moment their eyes locked. Layne's arms were yearning to enfold her. He imagined the softness of her lips on her own. A strange, magnetic force strove to pull the young couple together, but neither was sure of what the other was feeling.

To ward off an awkward moment, Connie said, "It's

been a wonderful evening, Layne. I can't tell you how much I have enjoyed it."

"Me, too." He grinned. "It has been an honor to be your escort. How soon is the next dance? Would you go with me again?"

"It's a month away," replied Connie, "but it's a date."

"A whole month?"

"Mmm-hmm."

"I'd sure like to see you before then."

"I'm certain that could be arranged."

"How about tomorrow?"

"Well, I—"

"Would you like to ride out to the ranch with me? I'm going to do a little fence mending. Won't take real long."

"Tomorrow is Sunday," Connie said thoughtfully. "I really ought to be at services. But I could ride out to the ranch and meet you when church is over."

"I'm in no particular hurry," Layne said quickly. "It's . . . uh . . . been a long time since I've been to church. Probably be good for me."

"Wonderful!" breathed Connie. "I'll fix up a picnic lunch, and you can ride one of our horses."

Again Layne Britton felt the urge to take the lovely woman into his arms and kiss her, but he resisted. He would not risk her thinking him too bold.

Connie, also off balance, took both of his hands in hers, squeezed them, and said, "See you in the morning. Thanks for such a lovely evening." With that, she mounted the steps and entered the deep shadows of the porch. Opening the door, she paused and said, "Good night."

Layne bid her good night, turned, and walked away. Connie stood in the doorway, watching him fade from sight. As the sound of his footsteps died out, she stood in bewilderment, a curious warmth flooding through her heart. "Good night, Layne Britton," she whispered.

Chapter Nine

Connie closed the door and leaned her head against it. None of the young men she had dated before her mother's illness had affected her like this. She was astounded by how eagerly she had responded to Layne's touch as his powerful arms had swept her up and away across the dance floor.

Slowly she turned, walked down the hall, and began climbing the stairs. As she thought of the plans for the next day, she realized that she could not anticipate being with Layne again without a tingle of excitement.

Approaching her room, she noticed there was light under Dolph's Catron's door. Quietly, she entered her bedroom and closed the door. Within moments she had two lanterns going. The room seemed stuffy, so she raised both windows a few inches. Dreamily she sat on the edge of the bed and stared off into space. Losing track of time, she reviewed the evening spent with the gentle, handsome man.

Suddenly, a distant sound cut into Connie Lee's thoughts. She went over to one of the windows, opened it farther, and listened. The sound came again. This time it was unmistakable. There was an excited crowd of people gathered over on Douglas Avenue, and the noise was gaining volume by the minute.

Connie heard Catron's door open, followed by his heavy footsteps moving down the hall. She darted to the door and stepped out just as he reached the stairs. He paused to look back.

"Are you going over to see what the excitement is about?" Connie asked.

Catron nodded and started down the stairs.

"Wait!" she cried. "I'm going with you!"

After Layne Britton had bid Connie good night, he headed toward Douglas Avenue, his heart in a whirl. This stunning young woman had him in a daze. As the lanterns of Wichita's principal street came into view, he thought of how light and delicate she had felt in his arms while the music played. He pictured her again—the full skirt and fitted bodice that emphasized her shapeliness, the coal-black ringlets that danced and adorned her elegant face, the light and graceful movements that enhanced her femininity. Layne could barely wait to see her again.

Douglas Avenue was thick with people as Layne came around the corner and headed toward the Sunflower Hotel. After a few steps, he moved off the sidewalk, angling across the broad street. Abruptly, like cockroaches coming out of the woodwork, Boone Foss and Dolph Catron's two henchmen filed out of the shadows and blocked his way.

Layne Britton halted, facing them.

Loudly, Boone Foss bellowed, "You ain't dodging me anymore, Britton! We're having a showdown here and now!"

People were stopping, gathering into clusters.

Layne's face stiffened and became cold as ice. Fixing Boone with a level, unblinking stare, he said, "I'm not even wearing a gun, Foss. I told you I'm through shedding blood."

Boone rolled back on his heels and laughed. "You sure are! Tonight I'm gonna shed *your* blood."

Layne eyed the growing crowd, then said, "You're not fast enough, sonny. But you'll never know it, because I'm not armed and we're not squaring off."

"You're a yellow-bellied sidewinder!" screamed Boone.

Anger leaped into Layne Britton's steel-gray eyes.
"The only reason I don't pound you into the dirt, Foss,"
he said gratingly, "is because you're a sawed-off runt.
Now get out of my way before you make me mad."

"No you don't!" lashed Boone. "With guns, size
don't make no difference. You ain't going nowhere till
you face me gun for gun!" Holding Layne with his wild
gaze, he motioned with his hand and said, "W. D., your
gunbelt will fit his waist. Give it to him!"

Stepping forward under the eyes of the crowd, W. D.
Hunt released the gunbelt from his body and extended it to
Layne Britton. Anger was vivid on Layne's face, but he
did not reach for it.

Suddenly, Boone Foss stepped up, grabbed the gunbelt
from Hunt, and thrust it into Layne's hand. "Strap it on,
yellow-belly!" he snarled.

Layne took it with a jerk, whipped the revolver from
its holster, and swung the barrel in a full arc. It met the
side of Boone Foss's head with a sodden sound. The
gunfighter hit the ground hard and lay still. Silence moved
like an invisible hand over the street.

Layne shoved the gun back in the holster and tossed it
at W. D. Hunt. Running his hot gaze over the two
henchmen, he hissed, "Pick up this chunk of buzzard bait
and get him out of here. Keep him out of my sight, do you
understand?"

Abruptly, Big Jack McQuaid stepped forward, peeling off his shirt. With his grizzly-bear voice, he growled,
"I ain't no sawed-off runt, Britton! And you're gonna
fight me!"

McQuaid swung his fist at Layne, hitting him hard in
the stomach before Layne had a chance to defend himself.
Layne doubled over in pain, but he quickly straightened
up, a look of loathing and uncontrollable rage in his eyes.

Layne was angry enough to take on both of Boone
Foss's friends at one time. He did not even flinch at the
massive size of Big Jack McQuaid. Layne and McQuaid
both stood six feet five inches in their boots, but McQuaid
was seventy pounds heavier. He had a huge head that was
set on a thick, bull-like neck and heavy rounded shoulders.

His arms resembled tree trunks, and his oversized hands became dangerous clubs when balled into fists. He was bulky through the waist, and his deep, rounded chest was a forest of coarse, wiry hair. Standing in the middle of the dusty street, McQuaid looked like an unmovable mountain.

While Big Jack paraded his massive frame around the edge of the crowd, the inflamed Layne Britton removed his gray Stetson. Nelda Monroe detached herself from the onlookers and said, "I'll take it, Mr. Britton." Layne nodded his thanks. Off came the fancy gray coat with the black piping, followed by the vest, the black string tie, and the white shirt, all of which he handed to Nelda.

Layne began working his arms, loosening the shoulder joints. Years of hard work had formed him perfectly. In contrast to McQuaid's thick middle, Layne Britton's broad shoulders tapered from a muscular chest to a hard, slim waist. As he moved his solid arms, the muscles in his broad back rippled and corded. Finally he entered the circle made by the crowd and glared heatedly at McQuaid.

Squaring with the well-proportioned man, McQuaid sloped his massive shoulders and roared, "I'm gonna beat you to a senseless pulp, Britton!" A look of cruel pleasure etched itself across his brutal face.

"Do it and *then* talk about it!" came the reply.

Instantly Layne Britton became rigid. There was no mistaking the meaning of the glitter that leaped into McQuaid's eyes. It meant battle. Although he had respect for the huge man's size and obvious power, Layne allowed himself no fear. He had fought giant-sized bullies before, and they always had a vulnerable spot. He would find McQuaid's.

The bulky monster came at Layne like a runaway freight train. Nimbly, Layne dodged Big Jack's pumping fists. McQuaid pivoted, slightly off balance, and Layne smashed him in the nose with a hissing right. The huge man stumbled, blinking at the rush of water to his eyes. Layne swung again, driving a piston-style punch to the same spot.

The crowd roared as blood appeared, and shock registered on McQuaid's reddening face.

McQuaid swore violently. Like a wild beast, he charged full-force. Layne slammed the bloody nose again, and it cracked like splitting wood. The huge man staggered slightly but kept on coming, then caught the ex-gunfighter with a savage fist in the stomach. Breath whooshed from Layne's mouth, and black dots danced in front of his eyes. Before he could recover from the blow, McQuaid caught him with an uppercut.

Layne felt his feet leave the earth and his back slam down. A wave of nausea swept over him as he saw the giant beast dropping toward him with knees aimed at his midsection. Layne rolled quickly and flipped to his feet. As McQuaid stood up, Layne saw the smear of blood on his face. The wide nose was bleeding profusely. *The nose! That's it,* thought Layne. *His vulnerable spot!*

Blood bubbled from McQuaid's nostrils as he swung a haymaker. Layne dodged and peppered his opponent's vulnerable spot with four straight lefts. He finished the flurry with a hard right to the jaw, then glided free of another wild swing. The crowd shouted its approval.

McQuaid roared like a wounded jungle beast and charged in again. Layne caught him with a right that partially glanced off. Jack's left fist connected squarely, and Layne went down. The excited throng began to scream for him to get up.

The giant rushed in and kicked Layne savagely in the ribs. Pain lanced Layne's rib cage, but he managed to seize the foot that kicked him and give it a fierce, violent twist. McQuaid yowled in agony and slammed to the hard surface of the street.

Layne leaped to his feet, fists poised. His ribs felt as if they were caved in. Big Jack was struggling to stand up, his foot and ankle hurting severely. Voices in the crowd were urging the tall stranger to finish him off.

In the few seconds it took McQuaid to gain his feet, Layne found Connie's face in the crowd. She stood between Nelda Monroe and Dolph Catron, her features pale and incredulous.

The monster was limping, but he stirred dust as he thundered at Layne Britton, swinging a meaty fist. Layne

ducked under it and slammed the bleeding nose without
mercy. McQuaid staggered and scowled blackly. "I'm
gonna break you in half!" he roared, eyes wild. He issued
a crowing cry and lowered his ponderous head to charge.

Layne stood his ground and, with a hissing uppercut,
popped Big Jack's head up, exposing the giant's midsection.
Layne then drove an ax blow into the man's stomach with
all of his weight behind it. Big Jack doubled over, gasping
and sucking in air. Layne stepped sideways and brought a
balled fist down with a sledgehammer blow on the back of
the huge man's bulky neck. McQuaid plopped flat on the
ground but immediately struggled to get up.

"On your feet, Jack!" shouted a man in the crowd.
"He's got some more for you!"

W. D. Hunt moved forward now, as if to come to his
partner's aid. But he felt an iron grip on his shoulder and
turned to see Marshal Roy Templeton, who said, "You
keep out of this, Hunt. This fight is between those two
men." Hunt got the message and faded back into the
crowd.

A white-faced woman turned to the marshal now and
said plaintively, "Marshal! Why don't you stop them?
Look at all the blood!"

"Why should I, Mrs. Carberry?" chortled the ample-
bellied lawman. "It's the *right* blood!"

Jack McQuaid was on his feet again, shaking his head
to clear it. He bared his teeth like a cornered wolf and
came at Layne in wild desperation. No man had ever done
this to the formidable giant. His breathing was like the
rattle of dry weeds in an autumn wind.

Layne met him, anger burning his veins like raw
whiskey. He ducked a swinging fist and slammed the nose
again. McQuaid staggered, his legs rubbery. Layne pounded
him with a left and a right. Big Jack's eyes resembled
polished glass. He stood, swaying like a palm tree in a
heavy breeze. Layne punched him again. Blackness swam
across the giant's eyes.

Layne set himself and swung a right with all his
weight behind it. The fist caught the giant flush on the
jaw, sounding like a flat rock dropping in mud. The huge

man's feet flew upward from the impact of the blow, and his immense frame smashed into the ground with an earth-shaking thud. Big Jack McQuaid was out cold.

The crowd sent up a round of cheers as Layne Britton made his way to a nearby horse trough, fell to his knees, and submerged his head in the water. When he stood up, water dripping, he eyed Boone Foss sitting on the edge of the board sidewalk, holding a wet cloth to his head.

Sucking hard for air, the tall man walked up to Boone and stood over him. The crowd quieted. Layne spoke with the difficult calm of a very angry man. With bitter hostility he hissed, "You stay out of my way, Foss! You hear me? Next time, I'll kill you!"

Big Jack McQuaid was still unconscious as Layne shuffled to where Nelda Monroe held his clothes. Connie stepped up and touched his arm. "Layne," she said, eyes full of worry, "are you all right?"

While Layne assured her he was okay, Dolph Catron slipped into the crowd, made a sly remark to W. D. Hunt, and went to his office.

People came to Layne Britton, congratulating him. He bid Connie good night and walked to the hotel, carrying his clothes and holding his ribs.

Within half an hour after the crowd had dispersed, Dolph Catron assembled in the windowless back room of his office with W. D. Hunt and the battered, puffy-faced Big Jack McQuaid.

Eyeing McQuaid with scorn, Catron said, "I'm not listening to you anymore, Jack. This Layne Britton is more man than you can handle, and I still say Britton could draw his gun three times before that stupid Foss could find the handle to his own."

McQuaid grunted something unintelligible. Catron ignored him and said, "Foss is a fool. He needs to be put out of the way. And Britton still threatens my project. He's got to be eliminated." Leaning close to W. D. Hunt, he added, "Now, *I* have a plan . . ."

*   *   *

Sunday morning came with the gray dawn giving way to a luxurious display of flaming orange-red, followed by a yellow sun lifting into a flawless blue sky.

At church services, Layne Britton was congratulated again for his handling of Big Jack McQuaid. Connie and Layne parted after church to change clothes. Dressed in his work clothes and straw hat, Layne left the hotel and walked to the Catron house.

Presently, the young couple rode out of the yard. Layne was on a chestnut gelding, and Connie, in form-fitting riding pants, rode her own bay mare. Layne carried the picnic basket, balancing it on the saddle pommel. Neither of the pair noticed that Dolph Catron watched them from an upstairs window.

Connie wore a white blouse that accentuated her black hair. Layne found her absolutely breathtaking.

As they left Wichita behind, Connie said, "Layne, we haven't talked of it yet today, but I want to say that I am proud of you. Nelda told me how you avoided killing Boone Foss." She paused momentarily, then asked, "You didn't really mean what you said to Foss after the fight, did you?"

"You mean about killing him next time?"

"Yes."

Looking a bit sheepish, he grinned. "No, Connie. I was just mad. I never want to kill anybody again. I'm just a peaceable rancher now."

Connie chuckled, "You didn't look very peaceable last night."

"Well," responded Layne, clearing his throat, "it's a mite difficult to fight for your life and be peaceable!"

Connie laughed. "There were times you looked like you were enjoying it."

"Well," said Layne defensively, "a good fight now and then is healthy for a man."

"Even when his ribs are kicked in?"

"They'll heal," he said dryly.

Both of them rode quietly for a while, then Layne said, "I know Dolph Catron is your stepfather, Connie. What about your real father?"

Connie turned her face away from Layne, biting her lip. He immediately realized he had touched a sore spot and said, "Oh, I'm sorry. I didn't mean to upset you."

"It's all right," she replied, facing him again. "Would you like to listen to a long, sad story?" Somehow Connie felt as if she had known Layne Britton all of her life. She wanted to share her burden with him. His very presence seemed to give her strength.

By the time they rode through the gate of the Kellogg ranch, Layne had heard the entire account of her mother's confession and all the related events, before and after. Connie told him about the letter Ozzie Gisler was carrying to Colonel Morgan Lee and of her apprehension about her father's reaction. Layne assured her that it would turn out all right.

"Well, if it does," she said as they dismounted at the barn, "I'll be making a trip to Dodge."

"Hope you won't be gone too long," he mused.

Connie did not know how to respond to his statement, so she said idly, "Can't be too long. I have a job waiting for me at Weneke's store."

Layne led the horses through the barn and into the corral, then closed the barn door. Stepping back into the sunlight, he said, "Are you going to stay at Catron's house?"

"No. We're barely on speaking terms. I've already arranged to move in with Nelda as soon as I start work."

Layne was pleased to hear that Connie was going to get away from Dolph Catron. "Tell you what," he said, getting off the subject, "let me show you the house. Then we can take the food out by the stream. The fence work I need to do is near there."

Connie agreed, and they walked to the house. As they entered, she sniffed lightly and said, "I love the smell of new paint." Gliding from room to room, she gave her approval of his restoration work.

"I'll be moving in within a couple of days," he said.

Connie fingered the faded curtains in the parlor and casually commented, "This house needs one thing."

"What's that?"

"A woman's touch," she answered, smiling up at him.

"How well I know," he agreed. There was a lull in the conversation, and Layne, feeling uncomfortable, returned to the kitchen.

Connie broke the silence by saying, "If you will permit me, Layne, I will make you new curtains for the whole house."

"I can't let you do that," he said, still struggling within. "That would be a lot of work."

"Oh, but I would love to do it," she insisted.

Looking into her eager eyes, he grinned and said, "Okay. But I'll pay for the material."

"It's a deal!" she exclaimed. "I'll come back with you tomorrow and measure the windows."

"In the meantime," said Layne, "I'm getting hungry!"

Together they strolled across the grassy field toward the tree-lined stream that lay to the northwest. Connie carried the picnic basket, while Layne bore tools and staples to repair the fence.

Finding a shady spot beside the stream, the couple sat down on the bank and enjoyed cold baked chicken, potato salad, and a berry pie. While they ate and chatted, Layne struggled with his emotions. Connie was feeling something for him. He could read it in her eyes.

No! he told himself. *I cannot allow myself to fall in love until I am once and for all rid of my gunfighter past. She cannot be expected to live with the constant threat of some gunfighter stalking me and destroying her life.*

After the meal, Connie followed Layne to the spot where the barbed wire sagged. She watched him while he worked. Suddenly she knew. There were only two things in the world she wanted: reconciliation with her father and the love of Layne Britton. There was no doubt about it. She had fallen in love with this man. He was everything a woman could desire. Kind, gentle, intelligent . . . yet rugged and manly. He had goals and a purpose in life. Connie knew Layne was strongly attracted to her, as well. She was sure of it, even as she watched him attempt to conceal it.

The three hours he labored with the fence seemed like only minutes to Connie. She was content just sharing time with Layne, and before she knew it, it was late in the afternoon.

They returned to the spot where they had eaten lunch. As Connie started to pick up the picnic basket, her eyes strayed to the cool water of the stream. Looking up at Layne, she said, "My feet are hot from all this walking. Would you mind if I soaked them for a few minutes?"

Layne sat beside Connie as she dabbled her bare feet in the water. They talked of various things until they both became aware that the sun was dropping low on the western horizon.

"We'd better head back," Layne said reluctantly.

When Connie had replaced the shoes on her feet, Layne stood up, and offered her his hand. He helped her up and their eyes met. Something magnetic pulled at them, and Layne Britton's defenses crumbled. He lowered his face toward hers.

A passion of yearning washed over Connie as she closed her eyes and his lips held hers in a lingering kiss. For a moment the two were lost in a world that seemed far removed from earth. They returned to reality when their lips parted, but neither could speak. Connie rested her head against his muscular chest, her senses reeling. She could hear the thunder of his heart as he pulled her tightly to him. Her own heart leaped in response.

After a time, while his strong arms still held her close, Layne said with feeling, "Connie, I can't do this to you."

"What do you mean?" she breathed.

"I am falling in love with you. I have tried to fight it, but it's bigger than I am."

Pressing against his arms until he released her, Connie looked up into his face. "I feel the same about you."

Closing his eyes, Layne gritted his teeth. "I can't let it happen, Connie. It isn't fair to you."

"I don't understand," she said, shaking her head.

"It's the brand that's on me," Layne sighed. "The

indelible mark of the gunfighter. If it isn't Boone Foss, it'll be some other young fool who's after me.''

"In time it will fade away,'' Connie said encouragingly.

"That's what I keep telling myself. But until it *is* gone, I can't offer you any kind of a life. It isn't fair."

"Fair?'' she echoed. "Don't I have a say in this?''

"Well, of course you do,'' he said tenderly, "but—''

Connie reached up and placed a forefinger on his lips. "If I am willing to take you just as you are, knowing that the mark is still on you, isn't that enough?''

Layne folded her hand into his own. "But you're young, beautiful, desirable. You could have any one of a hundred men in Wichita. Men who could give you a good life with no past to shadow it."

"You are overlooking one thing, Mr. Britton,'' she said levelly. "I'm not in love with a hundred men. I'm in love with you. Let me share your life. Let me help you live down your past. I want to be there, right by your side." Tears brimmed Connie's emerald eyes as she spoke.

"Oh, Connie, darling,'' he breathed. "That's what I want more than anything in the world.'' Gently he placed a finger beneath the curve of her chin. Layne took her face in both hands and tilted it up to his, holding it there briefly. Then he tenderly kissed each eyelid, the top of her nose, and finally pressed his lips to hers in a kiss of fiery passion.

Again, Layne held Connie close, breathing warmly into her ear. "At least I don't have to hide my love anymore,'' he said, ejecting a long sigh.

"You weren't hiding it,'' she said. "I saw it in your eyes.''

Neither spoke for a long moment. They just stood, enjoying the ecstasy of their young love.

Connie broke the silence. "Layne?''

"Yes?''

"When did you first begin to feel it?''

"The first moment I looked into your eyes when we passed on the street. When did *you* first feel it?'' he asked.

"Oh, it was a long time after that,'' she answered, with a teasing tone in her voice.

"Yeah?"

"Mmm-hmm. It didn't hit me until we'd passed and I reached the next corner!"

The happy couple laughed together, kissed again, and walked back to the house. Layne put the tools away and passed through the barn to fetch the horses.

Connie was waiting in the yard when she saw him return alone from the dark interior of the barn. "You're not going to believe this," he said, "but the horses are gone."

"Gone?" the woman gasped.

"Someone came in here and took them," he nodded. Looking at the brilliant sunset, he said, "It'll be dark when we get back to town, but all we can do is walk."

Chapter Ten

As Connie Lee and Layne Britton were walking toward town, Wichita's lamplighter was preparing to do his nightly job. The shadows on the dusky streets were growing darker. People were moving about on the boardwalks and in the street.

Under the canopy in front of the Broken Spur Saloon, the bruised Big Jack McQuaid sat on a bench talking with Boone Foss, who wore a bandage on his head where Layne had struck him with a gun. The tips of their cigarettes glowed red in the shadows.

Suddenly, a tall figure appeared directly across the street from the Broken Spur, wearing Layne Britton's Stetson and gray coat. His face was obscure in the dusk, but the clothing was easily identified. The man whipped out a revolver. At the same instant, McQuaid dived for cover, leaving the unsuspecting Boone Foss the only target. The orange muzzle flash of gunfire cut the gathering gloom as the sound of three shots clattered and echoed among the false-fronted buildings. Boone Foss jerked and spun as the bullets found their mark. As he toppled to the boardwalk, a woman screamed.

Looking shocked, McQuaid knelt beside the fallen gunfighter. The man in Layne Britton's clothes vanished into the shadows. As people began to crowd around Boone Foss, McQuaid yelled, "Somebody get Doc Wilson!"

A voice in the crowd advised them that Marshal Templeton was on his way.

"Is he dead, Jack?" someone asked.

"Too dark to see much," replied McQuaid, "but I can't feel a pulse."

As Templeton appeared on the scene, a man said, "It's Boone Foss, Marshal, and I seen who done it!"

"Me, too!" spoke up another. "It was Layne Britton! I'd know them fancy clothes anywhere!"

Several voices agreed: It was Layne Britton who shot down Boone Foss.

Another voice said, "We heard Britton threaten to kill him last night! You heard it, too, Marshal!"

Templeton nodded his agreement. Turning to Deputy Tom Olson, who had just appeared on the scene, he said, "Come with me, Tom. We're going to Britton's hotel room."

Dr. Wilson arrived, carrying his black bag and calling for someone to bring a lantern.

The two lawmen charged up the stairs at the Sunflower Hotel, guns drawn. The skinny hotel clerk followed halfway up the stairs and paused.

"Okay, Britton!" bellowed Templeton, banging on the door. "This is the marshal. Come on out!"

There was no response.

"Fred, come and open this door!" commanded the marshal.

Timidly, the clerk topped the stairs and handed Templeton the key. "You do it," he said, retreating down the stairs.

The marshal fumbled momentarily with the lock and then opened the door. Tom Olson followed him into the room and struck a match. Templeton looked around and said gruffly, "He isn't here, and neither are his fancy duds."

The two lawmen returned to the street to find that Boone Foss was still alive. Four men carried him to Doc Wilson's office.

"All right, men," spoke up Templeton, "I'll deputize every one of you here and now. First thing we're gonna do is search this town. Britton doesn't own a horse, so he'd have to steal one or get one from the livery. If he hasn't done either, then he's hiding somewhere close. All of you raise your right hands.''

While Roy Templeton was swearing in the deputies, W. D. Hunt slipped into the hotel from the alley door and made his way to Layne Britton's room. Using the same key he had used earlier—the one given him by the sweep boy, Danny Smith—he replaced the Stetson and the clothes in the room. Hurriedly, he left by the back way and joined the crowd of searchers, unnoticed.

Layne Britton and Connie Lee were less than a mile from town when they spied their horses tied to a tree beside the road. Breathing an oath, Layne said, ''If this is somebody's idea of a joke . . .''

Quickly the horses were untied, and the couple mounted up. ''This is quite unusual,'' agreed Connie, ''but I haven't minded the walk. It has given me more time with you.''

Layne pulled his horse close, placed a hand on the back of Connie's head, and kissed her tenderly. ''I haven't minded it either,'' he said warmly.

No one was on Market Street as Layne and Connie rode slowly into town. They put the horses in the Catron barn and walked to the porch.

''Thank you for a wonderful day,'' Connie said. She was physically exhausted, and the languor of her weariness softened her face.

The tall man moved close. ''I love you, Connie Lee,'' he said softly.

''And I love you, Layne Britton,'' she breathed. Her lips were drawn slightly apart by a warm smile when he kissed her. Connie's fingers found the back of his head and buried themselves in his hair.

Easing the pressure of his arms around her slender body, Layne studied Connie's beautiful face. He kissed her lightly and said, ''Good night. I'll see you tomorrow.''

Connie stood on the porch, her heart throbbing, and watched until the darkness swallowed his towering form.

Layne Britton felt as though he were walking on air. What a lucky man he was! He had the love of the most beautiful woman he had ever seen.

He was nearing the Sunflower, wondering why there was no one on the street, when two men jumped from the shadows, guns drawn. "Hold it right there, Britton!" one of them barked.

Layne halted, puzzlement in his eyes.

Cupping a hand beside his mouth, the same man shouted skyward, "We got him, Marshal! We have Britton in custody! Marshal-l-l! We got him!"

"What's going on?" asked Layne, as the sound of running footsteps came from every direction.

"You just don't move an eyelid, Britton!" warned the man. "The marshal will be here in a minute. You're under arrest!"

Layne's jaw slacked. "Arrest? What are you talking about?"

"Hey, Jasper!" came a voice from the gathering throng of men. "You got him!"

Layne looked around at the throng of predatory faces. "What is this?" he demanded.

Marshal Roy Templeton's voice boomed over the others as he elbowed his way through the crowd. "I'll handle it!" Moving in and facing the tall man, he snarled, "You're under arrest, Britton!"

"Marshal, what are you talking about?" asked Layne, temper rising.

"As if you didn't know," said Templeton. "I told you I didn't want any trouble in my town."

Layne bristled. "You talking about the fight last night?"

"Enough of this gibberish!" rasped Templeton, leveling his own gun on Layne. "Let's go!"

"Marshal," said Layne, standing his ground, "what is the charge?"

"All right," said Templeton angrily, "I'll spell it out for you. You're under arrest for the attempted murder of Boone Foss."

"Boone Foss? When did this happen?"

"Exactly one hour ago," came the marshal's reply. "Foss ain't dead yet. You'd better pray he lives."

"I was on Kellogg Road an hour ago," Layne said emphatically. "Connie Lee and I were together. We were coming back from my ranch."

"That's a dirty lie!" shouted a man in the crowd. "I saw you shoot down Foss with my own eyes! Changed clothes mighty fast, didn't you?"

Other voices concurred that they also had witnessed Layne shooting Boone.

"Didn't take you long, Britton!" came another voice. "We heard you tell Boone last night you were gonna kill him!"

"Something's haywire, here, Marshal," spoke up Britton. "Go ask Connie where we were an hour ago."

"I'll do just that!" snapped Templeton. Turning to Tom Olson, he said, "You take him over to the jail and lock him up."

The crowd of men followed Marshal Roy Templeton to the home of Dolph Catron. The stout-bodied attorney was on the porch smoking a cigar when they tromped into the yard. Standing up, Catron said, "You catch Britton, Marshal?"

"Sure did," nodded Templeton. "But he says he couldn't have shot Foss because he and your stepdaughter were riding in from the Kellogg ranch at the time Foss was shot."

"When did the shooting occur, Marshal?" It was the voice of Connie Lee. She had heard the crowd coming toward the house, and now stood in the open front door. She had changed into a long chenille robe.

"An hour and ten minutes ago," replied the marshal.

"Layne's telling you the truth," she said flatly.

"Huh?" Templeton said, jaw sagging.

"She's lying, Marshal!" shouted an unidentified man in the crowd. "I saw Britton shoot Foss myself!"

"What horses were you riding?" demanded Templeton.

"The chestnut and the bay," responded Connie, growing more perturbed.

Suddenly, Dolph Catron said heavily, "Marshal

Templeton, you know I am a law-abiding citizen in this town, and I wish we were rid of scum like Boone Foss. But if this Layne Britton would shoot the man down in cold blood, he's worse than Foss. I certainly hope you will see that Britton gets what's coming to him, to the fullest extent of the law.''

"You're a lawyer," said Templeton. "You know that's up to the judge and jury.''

Connie gasped, "Judge and jury?" Bolting from the doorway, she faced Templeton head-on. "What do you mean, judge and jury? I tell you Layne and I were together at the Kellogg ranch all afternoon. We didn't get back to town till less than half an hour ago!"

Dolph Catron turned toward Connie in the light that came from inside the house. Looking at her shamefully, he said, "Now, Connie, just because you're sweet on this disreputable gunfighter doesn't mean you should lie for him.''

The girl's mouth popped open. She gasped a breath, eyes wide, and said with conviction, "I'm not lying!''

Abruptly, a man pushed his way through the crowd and said, "Marshal, I just checked the chestnut and the bay in the barn. Neither one is sweaty. If them two had been riding all the way from the Kellogg ranch as she says, they'd still be hot.''

"We didn't ride them all the way!" said Connie, her voice on the edge of anger. "Someone took the horses from the corral at the Kellogg place this afternoon. We had to walk nearly all the way. We found them tied to a tree just outside of town and rode them in.''

"Connie," said Catron, touching her arm, "you mustn't—''

Jerking her arm loose, Connie hissed, "Don't you touch me!" Flicking her eyes to Templeton, she said, "Marshal, I'm telling you the truth! Layne Britton was with me at the time you say Boone Foss was shot. He couldn't have done it!''

Dolph Catron looked at Roy Templeton, his face a picture of honesty, and said, "The girl is lying. She has been in the house since midafternoon. She has not gone out the door.''

Connie was so angry she could not speak and could only glare at Catron with burning contempt.

Templeton looked past Connie Lee's furious eyes and said to Catron, "Doc Wilson says it's touch and go with Boone Foss. If he lives, Britton will get fifteen to twenty. If he dies, we'll be having us a hanging."

Connie's temper reached its limit. "Layne Britton is innocent, I tell you!" she screamed at Templeton.

"The jury will decide that," the marshal said tonelessly.

The furious Connie stormed into the house and ran upstairs to her room. Moments later, she emerged from the room, again in her riding outfit. As she reached the bottom of the stairs, Dolph Catron stood in her way.

"Where are you going?" he demanded.

"None of your business!" she snapped, eyes flashing.

"Go back to your room," Catron said with a tone of authority.

Through clenched teeth, the angry woman said, "Don't tell me what to do, Dolph Catron!" With that she pushed past him and bounded out the door.

In the sudden silence, Dolph Catron grinned smugly. What could Connie do? Layne Britton was in a trap, and no one could spring him.

Connie was refused entrance to the jail. The marshal told her that visiting hours were over at five o'clock. She would have to come back in the morning. From there she went to the home of another Wichita attorney. Justin Barry was young and just getting started. He was eager to take on Layne Britton's case and said he would see Layne first thing in the morning.

Too angry to stay in the same house with Dolph Catron, Connie walked to Nelda Monroe's and spent the night with her.

The sun hid behind a dark bank of clouds the next morning. It seemed fitting to Connie. Three times she went to the jail and was turned away. First, it was before visiting hours. The second time, attorney Justin Barry was with Layne. The third time, Layne was being arraigned at the courthouse before Judge Hubert Lockridge.

At ten o'clock, Connie was finally allowed inside the jail. Deputy Tom Olson would give her fifteen minutes with Layne Britton, but she would have to talk to him through the bars of his cell.

The jail, as usual, was full. Each of the three cells held four men. With Layne was Sid Gilbert and two other drunks sleeping it off. Gilbert had come to, and he was sitting on the floor of the cell.

As Connie entered the cell area, whistles and catcalls filled the place. When Layne spied her, he reached through the bars, whispering her name. Connie grasped his hands, saying, "Oh, Layne, this is awful!"

"Honey, you shouldn't have come in here," Layne said, running his eyes over the motley crowd of prisoners.

"I had to see you," breathed Connie. "I tried to see you last night, but the marshal wouldn't let me in. This is my fourth attempt this morning. Justin Barry was here?"

"Yes. Thank you for sending him. He went with me to the arraignment."

"And?"

"The judge set my trial for Thursday."

"What does Justin think?" Connie asked, studying his eyes.

Layne's features grayed. "Looks pretty bad."

"But you're innocent!" she gasped.

"Somebody set me up, Connie," Layne said glumly. "The man who shot Foss was wearing my Stetson and my dress clothes. Tom Olson says they were not in my room when he and Templeton went there right after the shooting. Olson went back this morning. The hat and clothes have been returned."

"I assume Justin told you about Dolph lying to the marshal?"

"Yes. I'm sorry, but I think he's the one who set me up."

Jutting her jaw, Connie said, "Now that I've seen him for what he is, I know he's capable of it. But *why*?"

"Only one possible reason. He must have plans to get

his hands on my ranch. There is a deadline in the will. If I don't claim it by October twenty-eighth, it goes up for sale. Since Catron's handling the papers, he could easily sell it to himself . . . cheap.''

"And you were supposed to lay claim in his office today,'' Connie said anxiously.

"Yes. If Boone Foss dies, I hang. If he lives, Barry says I could get up to twenty years for attempted murder. Too many people think they saw me shoot Foss.''

Connie's lips began to quiver, and tears filmed her eyes. "Oh, Layne, there's got to be a way to prove your innocence!''

"My only hope was your testimony,'' he said despairingly. "But in that courtroom it's going to be your word against Catron's.''

"Maybe the jury will believe *me*,'' she said hopefully.

"Not with a whole passel of Wichita's responsible citizens swearing they saw me commit the crime. Besides, Justin Barry says Catron has this town in his hip pocket. The jury will believe him.''

"If only we had met someone on the road,'' Connie said ruefully. "If only someone had seen us.''

Abruptly Deputy Tom Olson appeared. Drawing near to the couple, he said, "Mr. Britton, Doc Wilson just stopped by. Boone Foss is going to live. Thought you would want to know.''

Connie ejected a tiny moan and half whispered, "Oh, thank God!''

Relief swept over Layne Britton's face. "That *is* good news, Deputy. Thank you.''

Olson smiled at Connie and said, "The marshal is still out. He's a stickler on visiting time, but since he's not here, you can start your fifteen minutes again.''

"Thank you, Tom,'' said Connie, returning the smile.

Sid Gilbert wobbled to his feet. Gripping the bars, he said, "Hey, Tom. When do I get out of here?''

"Have you forgotten already, Sid?'' asked Olson. "This time you pitched rocks through three windows on North Main.''

Droopy-eyed, the lush said, "I did?''

"You did. You're in for thirty days."

Gilbert mumbled an unintelligible word, turned, and sat down on the floor.

As Olson disappeared through the door, Connie squeezed Layne's hands and said, "Boone Foss is going to live. That's one piece of good news."

Layne sighed. "At least they won't hang me."

"You're not going to prison, either," she said resolutely.

"I wish you were right," he replied, shaking his head.

"Darling, you are innocent," Connie insisted. "You just can't go to prison for a crime you didn't commit!"

"It's happened before," he said dejectedly.

Connie raised a hand to his face and stroked it lovingly. With emotion rising in her voice, she said, "Something has got to happen! We've just found each other. They can't tear us apart now!" Tears filled her lovely eyes. "Oh, Layne, I love you!"

"I love you, too, honey," said the tall man.

"Whooee!" shouted a prisoner in the next cell. "Listen to that!"

"Shut up, Nate!" snapped one of his cell mates. "Leave them alone."

Lowering his voice, Layne said, "Connie, if I am convicted and sent to prison, you must find someone else. You have a right to some happiness. Especially after all these years of caring for your mother."

Pain contorted Connie's comely features. Brow knitted, she said, "My only happiness is loving you. I don't want someone else."

"But Connie, you—"

"I'll wait for you," she cut in. "If you go to prison, I'll wait for you!"

"But it isn't fair!"

"There you go again, Layne Britton," Connie said, looking him square in the eye. "I'm not concerned with what is fair. I love you, my darling. I will always love you. We were meant for each other. We will have each other. Even if we have to wait."

"But Connie—"

"I must go now, darling. I will be back later." Standing on her tiptoes, she kissed him lightly through the bars. "I love you," she whispered, and was gone.

One of the prisoners spoke up from across the room, "That's some woman you've got there, fella."

Layne Britton could only sigh.

Connie left the jail and went directly to Dolph Catron's office. She approached Len Cummings, Catron's assistant, and said snappishly, "Dolph in his office?" While she spoke, she was already moving toward Catron's door.

Cummings rose to his feet, saying, "Yes, but it would be best if you let me announce—"

Unceremoniously, Connie bolted through the door. The breeze caused by its swift opening fluttered papers from Catron's desk to the floor. The stout-bodied man looked up through a cloud of cigar smoke. Catron eyed her nonchalantly and said, "It's polite to knock."

"I don't feel very polite," Connie rasped. "I want to talk to you."

Looking at her with disdain, he said, "Talk."

From the outer office, Len Cummings closed the door behind Connie as she glared at her stepfather. A seething mixture of scorn, contempt, disgust, and fighting rage showed in her eyes. "You'll never get away with it!" she half shouted through her bared teeth.

Dolph Catron pulled the cigar from his mouth and studied its smoking tip. Calmly, he said, "Wanna bet?"

"What kind of inhuman beast are you?" Connie hissed.

"The kind who gets what he wants," he replied, placing the cigar between his teeth. His heavy jowls flushed slightly, and his narrowed eyes held a wicked look of triumph. "And there's nothing you can do about it."

Clipping the words between her teeth, Connie said, "You'll have to perjure yourself in court to do it, because I'm going to tell the truth!"

"Who'll believe you? The jury will see you as a love-struck female who's willing to lie to save her lover."

Connie's burning eyes focused on Catron as she said rapidly, "You are disgusting. You'd let an innocent man waste away in prison just to get your clammy fingers on a few more dollars!''

Ejecting a huge billow of smoke, Catron said, ''What is Layne Britton to you? You've only known him a few days. Forget him. There are plenty more men around. With your looks you can have your pick of the lot.''

For a moment Connie's anger blanked her mind. She wrestled for the proper words.

Rising from his chair, Dolph Catron laid the burning cigar in an ashtray. Rounding the desk toward her, he pressed his thick lips into a smile. ''Really, honey,'' he said sweetly, ''I've thought a lot about us lately.''

Connie stared at him incredulously. ''Us?''

''With me, you could have anything you want.''

The girl's back straightened. A wild flash of anger bolted from her eyes. ''With *you*?''

Reaching toward her, Dolph said, ''Connie, ever since you started to mature, I could hardly keep my eyes off you. I want you. We could wait a proper length of time, then we could marry. I—''

Raw flame ignited in Connie's eyes. Backing from his reach, she made a gagging sound in her throat. Catron took another step toward her, his lips puckered.

Choking the words out, she said, ''You make me sick!'' At the same instant, she seized the smoking cigar from the desk and stabbed the burning tip to his lips. The ponderous man howled and leaped backward, flinging a hand to his blistered mouth and singed mustache. Before he could recover his balance, Connie slammed the door behind her with blinding rage.

Chapter Eleven

It was just past noon when the Wells Fargo stagecoach rolled into Dodge City in a cloud of dust. Ozzie Gisler sat straight-backed on the box, the leathers between his callused fingers. Pulling the vehicle to a halt in front of the stage-line office, he told his shotgunner to hustle with the baggage. He would be back in time to pull out. Then he hurried to the livery stable across the sun-bleached street, rented a horse, and galloped westward.

Fort Dodge was five miles from the town. On the east side behind a five-foot wooden fence lay three long, narrow, L-shaped barracks. At the north of the compound were six peak-roofed structures that housed the officers. Just west of these was the hospital. The prison building stood alone near the west fence some sixty yards south of the hospital. The commandant's house, a two-story white building, was in the center of the compound, directly across the parade ground from the barracks. There were gates at all four corners, allowing the cavalry quick and easy access to the outside.

Ozzie Gisler pulled the horse to a stop at the southeast gate. A blue-uniformed soldier cautiously eyed him without a word.

"I'd like to see Colonel Morgan Lee," Ozzie said, painting on a smile.

"Is the commandant expecting you?" queried the guard.

127

"No, sir," replied Ozzie. "I'm an old friend. Name of Ozzie Gisler."

"Would you state your business, please?" asked the stern-faced guard.

"Well, I'm a stage driver for Wells Fargo," Ozzie said, a bit perturbed. "I drive the run between Dodge and Wichita."

"I did not refer to your employment, Mr. Gizzard," said the guard in a level tone. "What is your business with Colonel Lee?"

Ozzie had little patience with a man who could not smile. He figured anyone who took life that seriously might as well be dead already. He had commented to Bill Henderson once that a corpse never grins.

Maintaining his own smile, he replied, "I have a personal message for the colonel from his daughter in Wichita."

"I was not aware that Colonel Lee had a daughter," said the guard stiffly.

Fighting to retain his composure, Ozzie said, "You're probably also not aware that it takes thirty-seven muscles in your face to frown and only sixteen to smile, but it's a scientific fact. Other than that, there are four things you need to know. They come in this order: Colonel Lee has a daughter. I have a message from her to him. I'm in a dad-blamed hurry. And my name ain't Gizzard. It's *Gisler*."

"If you will give me the message," said the stone-faced soldier, "I will take it to the colonel."

"Nope," said Ozzie, shaking his head. "I was instructed by Miss Lee to plant it personally in the colonel's hand. Now, like I said, I'm in a hurry. If you delay me any more, I'll have to report you to the colonel."

Swinging the gate open, the stoical man said, "Colonel's quarters are across the parade from the barracks. Big house under the cottonwoods."

"Thank you," Ozzie replied, prodding his horse through the gate.

The commandant's house had a low porch running its breadth. The porch roof was supported by several southern-style white pillars. Dismounting, Ozzie stepped onto the shady porch and knocked on the door. He could make out a vestibule where a uniformed man sat behind a desk.

"Come in, sir," said the soldier.

As Ozzie entered, the man stood, smiling amiably, and said, "I'm Corporal Stram, Colonel Lee's secretary. May I help you?"

"First thing you can do is get that guard at the southeast gate a bottle of friendly elixir," cracked Ozzie, throwing a thumb over his shoulder.

Stram chuckled. "Peabody? Oh, he just takes his job too seriously."

"Acts like he's got a burr stuck in the trapdoor of his longjohns," Ozzie said dryly. "Second thing is that I need to see Colonel Lee on urgent business. I'm Ozzie Gisler, from Wichita. The colonel knows me."

"The colonel is in conference at the moment," Stram said, pointing at a closed door with his head. "You can see him as soon as he's finished. Just make yourself comfortable in one of those chairs."

"I don't suppose there's a way to hurry things along. I'm driver of the Wells Fargo stage. Gotta head for Wichita shortly. Already gonna be late because of that molasses-brained guard."

"I'm sorry, Mr. Gisler," said the corporal, "but there's nothing I can do. Is there a message I can—"

Suddenly the office door came open. A soldier ushered out a sullen-faced man who wore tattered clothing and handcuffs. As they left, Stram stepped to the office door and said, "Colonel, there's a gentleman out here to see you. Says he's from Wichita. His name is Ozzie Gisler."

Colonel Morgan Lee's familiar voice thundered through the open door, "Ozzie Gisler? He's no gentleman, Corporal! Tell him I said he's a snaggle-toothed old rascal!"

Ozzie countered instantly, and just as loud, "Tell the colonel I said he's a bowlegged buzzard who couldn't hit the butt end of a bloated bull with a banjo!"

Fort Dodge's commandant appeared in the doorway. In his early fifties, his full head of hair was nearly all gray, with mustache to match. Though deep lines ran across his forehead, he was still strikingly handsome. His stocky frame and thick shoulders were carried in a military manner, with head held erect. A warm, affectionate smile graced Morgan's face as he laid his green eyes on the lanky stage driver. "Hello, you old rascal!" he said, opening his arms.

"Howdy, buzzard!" responded Ozzie as the two men embraced and slapped each other on the back.

The colonel led Ozzie into his office and closed the door. Eyeing Ozzie's weather-worn features, he chuckled. "You don't look a day older than the last time I saw you. You still look ninety-nine!"

Ozzie laughed. "And you're just as ornery as ever!"

"I heard you were driving for Wells Fargo," said Morgan. "Still at it?"

"Yep. Been makin' the run between Wichita and Dodge."

"And you haven't come out here to see me?"

"Well," said Ozzie, his face darkening, "the schedule demands I take on fresh horses and turn right around and head back."

"But today is different?"

"Well . . . uh . . . yeah. I came out here today on a special mission." Ozzie reached inside his shirt. Pulling out an envelope, he grinned and said, "I have a letter for you from Connie."

"Connie?" echoed Morgan, jerking up his chin. He stared at the envelope in utter shock and disbelief.

Extending it to the astounded man, Ozzie said, "She asked me to deliver it personally and put it in your hand."

Morgan Lee took the envelope like a man in a dream. "Then you've seen her recently? She's still living in Wichita?"

"Yes to both questions," replied the old driver.

"How is she?"

"Just fine." Ozzie grinned. "And without taintin' the truth, Morg, she has turned out to be the most beautiful woman in the whole world!"

"Is . . . is she married yet?"

"Nope. She's had plenty of offers, but she's been all

tied up taking care of Cora for the past three years. But now that Cora's gone, she—''

"Cora?" cut in Lee.

"Oh, I guess you ain't heard yet," fumbled Ozzie. "Cora died last week. TB, you know."

The colonel nodded solemnly, a stunned look on his face. "I had heard she had tuberculosis. But I didn't know of her death."

Morgan bowed his head for a moment, staring silently at the letter in his hand. Footsteps could be heard outside, and distant voices, as Ozzie waited for the colonel to digest this news. After several minutes Morgan looked up and said, "Where is Connie staying now? She's not with Catron, is she?"

"She'll be staying with Nelda Monroe now," Ozzie said. "She's doin' just fine."

"I should have been there with her when her mother . . .'' Morgan shook his head and sighed, then looked up at Ozzie. "Thank you for bringing me this, Ozzie.''

I'm glad to, Morg. I'm afraid I'm already running late. I gotta get back to town." Gripping Morgan's hand, he added, "I hope that letter makes you real happy."

"I hope so, too," Morgan said. "It's sure good to see you again."

"Same here. And maybe it won't be so long till I see you next time."

The square-shouldered colonel crossed the vestibule and watched Ozzie Gisler ride away. Turning to his secretary, he said, "Corporal, I am not to be disturbed until I tell you differently."

"Yes, sir," nodded Stram.

Morgan Lee closed the door behind him, crossed the room, and sat down at his desk. With shaky fingers, he slit the envelope with a letter opener and pulled out the two folded pages. His heart raced as he spread them open and began to read.

Tears filled his eyes the instant he read the tender salutation. As his line of sight moved slowly from word to word, his vision blurred. Producing a white handkerchief from his hip pocket, he dabbed at his eyes as he read the letter.

On Tuesday morning, Connie left the jail after visiting Layne. Her heart was heavy with the prospect of the man she loved being sent to prison.

Two of Herman Weneke's sons at that moment were moving all of Connie's possessions from her former home to Nelda Monroe's place. Connie would not spend another day in Dolph Catron's house.

As Connie made her way up the boardwalk, she suddenly heard Ed Trask calling from the open door of the telegraph office, "Miss Connie! Oh, Miss Connie!"

Looking up, she answered, "Yes, Eddie?"

"A telegram just came for you! From Fort Dodge!"

Connie's heart leaped within her. Lifting her full-length skirt a few inches, she ran toward Trask.

Handing her the folded piece of paper, Trask said, "I think you'll like this."

With trembling fingers, Connie accepted the telegram. Opening it quickly, her eyes misted as she read it.

Darling Daughter Connie,
     Have your letter STOP Understand completely STOP Have paid your fare at Fargo office here STOP Please come on next stage STOP Love you more than ever STOP

Daddy

The overjoyed woman burst into tears. Pivoting, she hurried to the Wells Fargo office, securing a place on Ozzie Gisler's stagecoach for Saturday's run. Rushing back to the telegraph office, she wired Morgan Lee that she would arrive in Dodge City on Monday.

Moments later, Connie arrived at the jail, out of breath. As she entered the office, Marshal Roy Templeton stood up behind his desk and said, "Now, Miss Connie, you were here just a little while ago. I can't let you stay here with Britton all the time."

"I must see him only for a moment, Marshal," she said pleadingly. "You must let me."

"All right," he said, "but make it snappy."

Connie dashed into the cell area, and Layne Britton rose from the bunk to meet her. There was more room in the barred cubicle now. He shared the cell only with Sid Gilbert, who was stretched out on the other bunk. Gilbert listened as Connie said to Layne, "Darling, I just received a telegram from Daddy!" Thrusting it through the bars, she added, "Here, read it."

Layne's face lit up as he read Morgan Lee's message. "Oh, that's wonderful, Connie!" Looking into her tear-brimmed eyes, he said, "You *are* going on the next stage, aren't you?"

"Yes!" she beamed. "This could be such a happy occasion if only—" Her face clouded. "If only you—"

"Now, honey," Layne said, reaching through the bars and squeezing her hand, "don't let my situation mar your joy. Just think of it! After all these years, you and your father will have each other again."

Biting her lower lip, Connie said, "But if you go to prison—"

"If I do, honey, it will be Fort Dodge. At least . . . at least . . . well, since your father is commandant at the fort, you could see me when you come to visit him."

"Oh, Layne," she sniffed. "It just can't happen. You just can't go to prison. You're innocent. You—"

Placing the tips of his fingers under Connie's graceful chin, the tall man said firmly, "Chin up, darling. We can't have Colonel Morgan Lee's daughter in the doldrums. Your father loves you and wants to see you. Besides . . . this old jailbird loves you, too."

"And I love you," she said, tiptoeing to kiss him through the bars.

Sid Gilbert waited until Connie Lee had been gone over an hour before he made his move. He did not want to arouse Layne Britton's suspicion. Stepping to the bars while Layne lay on his bunk reading a week-old newspaper, Gilbert called out, "Hey, Marshal!"

Presently, Deputy Tom Olson appeared. "What is it, Sid?" he asked with an annoyed tone.

"Would you put out the word at the Big Buffalo Saloon that I need to see Cole Clinger? That's where he hangs out when he's in town."

"I'll see what I can do," droned Olson.

"Now, it's important, boy!" exclaimed Gilbert, catching the deputy's noncommittal tone.

"Like I said," came Olson's reluctant reply, "I'll see what I can do."

Sid Gilbert eyed the deputy warily as he left the cell area. Then he returned to his bunk. Sitting silently, he stared into space, deep in thought. Unwittingly, Connie Lee and Layne Britton had just given him the key to entrance into Cole Clinger's gang.

Clinger had been an outlaw leader for many years. Sid Gilbert knew that Charlie Prior, one of the old gang members, was imprisoned at Fort Dodge on a life sentence. He had saved Cole's life once in a train robbery, and the outlaw leader felt a debt to Prior. Sid had often heard him speak of trying to figure a way to break him out of prison. Excitement ran through Sid Gilbert's body. When Cole heard his plan, he would welcome Sid into the gang.

Breaking the silence in the cell, Gilbert spoke to Layne Britton. "Say, old buddy, do you mind if I look at part of that there newspaper?"

"It's as much yours as it is mine," answered Layne, tossing him a section he had already finished reading.

Sid Gilbert made as if he were reading the newspaper. Stealthily, he tore a corner from one page. Eyeing Britton carefully while he did it, Gilbert slipped a pencil stub from his pocket and wrote on the margin of the torn corner, *Come and see me Thursday while Britton is at the trial. I have good news.*

It was late afternoon when Cole Clinger showed up at the jail. Clinger entered the cell area, ran his dark eyes over the inmates, then spied Sid Gilbert asleep on his bunk. Moving close and pressing his face to the bars, he looked at Layne Britton.

"Hello, Layne," said the outlaw.

"Cole," nodded Layne, without expression.

Grinning indolently, Clinger said, "Got yourself into a mess, didn't you?"

"It is a little sticky," admitted the ex-gunfighter.

Cole looked toward the door to the office, swung his gaze back to Layne, and lowered his voice. "You want me to bust you out of here? Wouldn't be hard. That tinhorn Templeton is so stupid he couldn't find a frightened polecat in a chicken house."

"No thanks, Cole," said Layne.

"Make you a partner," offered Clinger.

"Not my cup of tea," grinned the tall man.

"Rotting in prison *is*?"

"No, but if I broke out of here, I'd be on the dodge the rest of my life."

Clinger shrugged his shoulders, lifted his voice, and hollered at the sleeping Gilbert, "Hey, Sid! Wake up!"

Wichita's town drunk snorted, rolled over, and sat up. Focusing his bloodshot eyes on Clinger's unattractive face, he ran a hand into a pants pocket, then stood to his feet. Moving to the bars, he reached out to shake the outlaw's hand.

Cole Clinger felt the folded piece of newspaper press his palm as he met Gilbert's grip.

"Glad you came, old pal," said Sid, a furtive look in his eyes.

Clinger got the signal, put the paper in his pocket, and said, "What'd you want, Sid?"

The lush said in a half whisper, "Could you smuggle me in a small bottle? I'm terrible thirsty."

Layne Britton looked at Cole and shook his head, smiling.

"I'll see," whispered Clinger. "May take a little doing, but I'll try."

Thursday morning at nine o'clock, the courtroom was jammed as Judge Hubert Lockridge entered in his black, flowing robe.

Layne Britton sat at a small table beside his attorney,

Justin Barry. The jury of twelve men sat in straight-backed chairs on a side platform, facing the judge's bench. The Sedgwick County prosecutor was a middle-aged man named Albert Neal. Among the crowd were Jack McQuaid and W. D. Hunt. Bill Henderson was there, sitting beside Betty Ann Stewart. Next to Betty Ann was a pallid-faced Connie Lee. On Connie's other side sat Nelda Monroe. Dolph Catron sat directly behind them. Doc Wilson was on hand to testify on Boone Foss's condition, with Marshal Roy Templeton seated next to him. Near the back of the room, Danny Smith sat between two elderly women.

The silver-haired judge tapped his gavel on the desk and declared the court in session. Albert Neal began by reading the official document charging Layne Britton with the shooting of Boone Foss.

By eleven o'clock, seven witnesses had testified that they saw Layne Britton gun down the victim. Justin Barry's cross-examination could not make even one witness admit that it was too dark to see the face of the man who shot Boone Foss. Each one was positive the would-be killer was the famous gunfighter. The reality of a prison term loomed heavily over Layne Britton after the noon break, as nineteen witnesses, including Marshal Templeton, testified to hearing the defendant threaten to kill Boone Foss after his fight with Jack McQuaid.

Connie took the stand and told of the missing horses and of the couple's long walk from the Kellogg ranch back to town. The all-male jury began to sway as the beautiful woman gave her story. However, Connie's testimony was nullified when Dolph Catron took the stand. Under Albert Neal's questioning, he looked straight at Connie and said, "Mr. Neal, I can understand Connie's infatuation for Britton. He is a mysterious, romantic figure of sorts, but to lie on this inviolable witness stand—"

"Your honor, I object to this man's remarks!" cried Justin Barry, leaping to his feet. "He is coloring the jury's thinking with insinuations that are cheap-shot opinions!"

The dour judge looked over his half-moon spectacles at Dolph Catron and said, "The witness will refrain from expressing his own opinions and give direct answers to the prosecutor's questions. You, of all people, should know this, Mr. Catron, being an attorney yourself.''

Catron's heavy neck reddened against his white collar. "I . . . uh . . . I apologize, Your Honor," he said, feigning contrition. "I am sorry." The unscrupulous man laughed within himself, knowing the damage was done. Looking at the prosecutor, he spoke heavily, somberly. "My stepdaughter returned home in the midafternoon on Sunday last and remained in the house the rest of the day."

Connie stared at him venomously. Fury ignited within her. Catron met her stare with a bland look of impassivity.

"Your witness," Neal said to Barry, stepping to his table and sitting down.

Justin Barry approached the stand and said, "Mr. Catron, you do live in a rather large house, I believe."

"Biggest in Wichita," the thick-bodied man said smugly.

"How many rooms are in the house?"

"Thirteen."

"Is it a two-story house?"

"Yes."

"Does anyone else live in the house with you and your stepdaughter, Connie Lee?"

"No. Not since my dear wife passed away."

"With such a large house, Mr. Catron," proceeded Barry, "would it not be possible for either of you to come and go without the other being aware of it?"

"Well, that could be, yes," conceded Catron.

Pointing to Connie, Barry said, "Miss Lee has testified under oath before this sovereign court that she was with the defendant all afternoon at the Kellogg ranch and did not return until after dark. Is it not possible, sir, that you thought she was in the house but were mistaken? I remind you, Mr. Catron, that the defendant stands to face severe punishment at the hands of the law. A simple conjecture on your part could result in a tragic miscarriage of justice."

Level-eyed, Dolph Catron filled the courtroom with his deep voice. "It is not conjecture, Mr. Barry. We were in the library from three o'clock on. Connie went upstairs after supper and changed into a robe. That's the way she was dressed when Marshal Templeton came to the house after the shooting Sunday evening."

Thunderous, uncontrollable rage possessed Connie Lee. The features of the men before her blurred as a crimson flush mounted her face. Hardly realizing it, she was on her feet, screaming, ejecting the words like a boiling maelstrom: *"Liar! Liar! Liar! Nothing but lies, Dolph Catron, and you know it! You'll let an innocent man go to prison just to satisfy your rotten greed! You set this whole thing up! You—"*

Suddenly the furious girl was aware of the judge banging the desk with his gavel, while Nelda and Betty Ann were speaking to her and pulling her down in the seat.

Judge Lockridge's stern voice was saying, "Another outburst like that, young woman, and you'll be removed from this courtroom!"

Connie did not apologize. She focused on Dolph Catron's repugnant face. He eyed her with supercilious scorn.

For the first time in her life, Connie Lee wished she were a man. The thought of rearranging Dolph Catron's facial features with bare knuckles was suddenly warm and pleasant.

While the trial was in session at the courthouse, Deputy Tom Olson allowed Cole Clinger to see Sid Gilbert. Two card games were going on in other cells, keeping the prisoners who were not sleeping occupied.

Clinger and Gilbert huddled face to face through the bars. Eyes bright and expressive, Gilbert said, "Cole, I got something special!"

"Spill it," the outlaw said levelly.

"I been telling you, Cole, you need me in your gang."

"Sure, sure," nodded Clinger. "What's this news you've got?"

"You been wanting a way to bust Charlie Prior out of the prison at Fort Dodge."

"Yeah."

"I got a surefire way for you to do it."

"Let's hear it."

"Oh, no, you don't. First you gotta promise that I can be part of your gang when I get outta here."

"If what you got is good, you're in," lied Clinger. "Now spill it."

The jury had been out the sum total of eight minutes when they filed back into the stuffy courtroom. Layne's chest went tight. Connie took Nelda's hand, squeezing down hard. Nelda's face was white under powder and rouge.

When the twelve men were seated, the judge said, "Gentlemen of the jury, have you reached a verdict?"

"We have," said the jury spokesman, rising to his feet. "We find the defendant, Layne Britton, *guilty as charged*."

Nelda wrapped her arms around Connie and held her tight. Layne's shoulders slumped. Dolph Catron sat in his place, a smug grin on his face.

Justin Barry whispered, "I'm sorry, Layne."

"Not your fault," said Layne. "Catron had the cards stacked against me from the beginning."

"The defendant will approach the bench for sentencing," said the somber-faced judge.

Justin Barry led his client to the bench.

"Layne Britton, you have been duly tried and convicted of attempted murder in this court of law. It is my duty to pass sentence upon you. A conviction of this sort may carry a sentence of five to twenty years in the territorial prison at Fort Dodge."

Connie sat frozen to the chair, Nelda still holding her tight.

"It is the judgment of this court that since you have no previous criminal record of any kind, the minimum sentence be enforced. You are sentenced to five years in the territorial prison at Fort Dodge, Kansas. You will be transported to that location at the discretion of Marshal Roy Templeton."

The gavel banged the desk, and the judge disappeared.

Connie rushed across the room to Layne. Folding her into his arms, he said, "Five years is a long time, darling. Time for you to find a young man, marry him, and start a family."

"How many times do I have to say it, Layne Britton?" she breathed, looking into his eyes. "If it had been twenty years, I would still wait for you. I love you. Do you understand?"

"Let's go, Britton," cut in Templeton.

"I understand," Layne said through tight lips. "I'll live for the day I'm a free man."

"We won't count time until then," Connie said softly. "We'll begin our lives the day you get out."

With the marshal pulling at his arm, Layne kissed her a final time.

Chapter Twelve

Ozzie Gisler had pulled his bright red stagecoach into Wichita while court was in session. The passengers had dispersed, and he was about to climb back aboard and pull away when he saw the crowd coming up the street from the courthouse. Spotting Connie and Nelda in the crowd as they passed, he followed them to Nelda's house.

As he caught up with the two women, Ozzie saw their wan faces and noticed the swelling around Connie's eyes. Puddles immediately jumped into Connie's arms when she saw her friend.

To Connie, he said, "What's this I hear about Layne goin' through some kind of court trial?"

Weeping, Connie ran into his arms, still cradling Puddles. Ozzie comforted Connie until she calmed down, and then the trio sat down on the porch. Connie gave him the whole story. When she told of Layne's five-year sentence, the old man's crinkled face turned beet-red. Gasping between words, he said, "Well . . . if . . . that . . . don't beat all. Why, that young fellow could no more be a . . . a murderer than I could! Of all the—"

Suddenly, he stomped out of the yard into the street and walked half a block. He halted in the middle of the street, swinging both fists violently. The two women watched, puzzled. They could hear the angry tone of his voice but could not make out the words. After several minutes, he wound down, took a deep breath, and returned.

141

Nelda asked, "What was that all about?"

"After what you told me, I'm d-d-d-dad-burned mad . . . and I had to cuss some of it out of my system. But I don't cuss in front of women!"

That night at the Big Buffalo Saloon, Cole Clinger met with four of his men. They sat around a large circular table that was well supplied with bottles and shot glasses. As a tinkling piano played across the room, Clinger ran his dark, piercing eyes over their faces.

His most trusted man was Lefty Scofield. Lefty was six feet tall and well built, with thick, square shoulders. Beside Lefty sat Leon Pelton. Leon was young—only nineteen—but a tough customer and handy with a gun. Next to Leon was Art Winkler. Somewhere in his forties, he was impetuous and hotheaded, but a good man to have around when there was trouble. Sitting next to Winkler was Frank Miller. Cold-blooded and heartless, he would kill at the drop of a hat.

Pouring himself a shot of whiskey, Clinger tossed it off in one gulp. Running the back of a hand over his mouth, he said, "I called you boys together because something special has come up. I'll fill the rest of the bunch in on it later."

"Big money job, boss?" asked Frank Miller.

"Not this time," said Clinger, lighting a cigarillo. "Mighty important, though. We're gonna spring Charlie Prior from prison."

The group was immediately interested.

"I found out today," he continued, "that a local gal named Connie Lee is daughter of Colonel Morgan Lee, commandant at Fort Dodge. She's taking the stage for Dodge on Saturday morning. Going to see her pa. Clinger laughed and blew smoke toward the ceiling. "But Miss Connie ain't gonna quite make it."

"How's it work, boss?" Lefty asked.

"I've already booked myself on the same stage," replied Clinger. "You boys and the rest of the gang will ride on ahead to Dodge. You'll wait off the side of the road at a place I know just this side of town. I'll take over the stage when we're drawing close to it.''

The outlaw leader downed another shot of whiskey, then continued. "When you see the stage pull over, you surround it. We'll hold the passengers and crew hostage. Our star hostage will be Connie Lee.''

"Hey, boss,'' spoke up Leon with a smirk. "Can I be the one to hold Connie?''

"I'll want her inside the coach. You can be her personal guard.''

"Playing favorites,'' complained Lefty sourly.

Clinger chuckled. "He ain't gonna do nothing but sit and look at her. Besides, Lefty, I've already got a job picked out for you. That girl's gonna write a note to the colonel. The note's gonna say that the man who hands it to the colonel must return with Charlie Prior immediately, or the first to die will be his own daughter. The man who carries the note in and brings Charlie out is you, Lefty.''

A wide grin spread over Lefty's unshaven face. "Okay, boss. I like that fine.''

Young Leon Pelton's face pinched. "Cole,'' he said worriedly, "you wouldn't really kill that beautiful woman, would you?''

"What's the matter, kid?'' growled Clinger. "You soft or something?''

"No, of course not,'' said Leon. "I don't mind killing a man if he's got it coming. But the Lee woman hasn't done anything to us. Besides, it would be a downright shame to do away with anything that pleasant on the eyes.''

Cole Clinger laughed. "Don't worry about it, kid. Her old man ain't gonna take no chances on losing his little girl. He'll produce Charlie, all right.''

Leon Pelton was still apprehensive. "But, Cole, if he does balk, what hap—''

"The woman dies!'' snapped Clinger, his face like granite.

"What if the colonel sends Charlie out, but comes after us with the cavalry?'' asked Art Winkler.

"We're keeping the woman till us and Charlie are

miles away," replied the outlaw leader. "She'll be turned loose when I feel it's safe."

"With that woman in our hands, ain't no cavalry gonna pull no shenanigans," put in Lefty.

"Right," agreed Clinger. Looking dead serious, he added, "I owe Charlie Prior my life. We're gonna get him out of that stinking prison. It'll be like old times with Charlie along, when we start robbing them trains."

While Cole Clinger prepared his men to carry out Charlie Prior's escape from the Fort Dodge prison, Ed Trask left the telegraph office and hurried along the dark street to Nelda Monroe's house. Connie responded to Trask's rapid knock. Swinging the door open, she knew something was wrong by the look in his eyes.

"Miss Connie," Trask said quickly, "is Miss Nelda here?"

"Yes," replied Connie, eyeing the folded paper in his hand. "She's on the back porch. I'll get her."

"I'm right here, honey," said the older woman, entering the room. "What is it, Ed?"

Soberly, Trask said, "Message just came from the telegraph office at Fort Dodge, ma'am. It's about your son."

Nelda took the paper from his hand, her brow furrowed. The color left her face as she read it.

The sun rose on Saturday morning with its silent burst of light heralding a new day.

Ozzie Gisler eyed the hard-featured face of Cole Clinger as the bright red coach rolled to a halt in front of the Wells Fargo office. Leaving Puddles in the seat, the wiry old man climbed down. He had learned from Harry Dunn that Clinger would be one of his passengers.

Ignoring Clinger, Ozzie crossed the boardwalk and entered the office. Two passengers, who had come in on the stage from St. Louis the previous day, waited in the office. They had spent the night at the Sunflower Hotel. One was Ted Drier, a fat patent-medicine salesman with a gift for gab. The other was Hattie Weems, a tiny, wrinkled woman of seventy-five.

"This is your driver, folks," said Dunn, nodding toward Ozzie.

"Howdy." Ozzie grinned, tipping his sweat-stained hat at the elderly woman. "I'm Ozzie Gisler."

"Hattie Weems is my name," said the tiny woman, with a voice that matched her size.

"Ted Drier," said the obese man, thrusting his hand into Ozzie's. "I'm in patent medicine."

"And I'm your shotgunner," came the voice of Bill Henderson as he emerged from a back room.

Ozzie's jaw dropped. Squinting at his friend, he said, "Billy, what are you doin' here? I thought Doc Wilson said you had to wait a couple more weeks!"

"He did," replied Bill, "but I can't stand sitting around. I'm not a hundred percent, but I'll be okay."

"Fine with me," said Ozzie. "I been missin' you."

Turning to the Wells Fargo agent, the wiry driver said, "Any more passengers sign up since yesterday?"

"You know about Nelda?" asked Dunn.

"Yep. I ate supper at her house yesterday. She told me about her son bein' so sick and all."

With a sly look, Harry Dunn said, "Seems you're spending more and more time at Nelda's."

Ozzie's face flushed. "Now look here, Harry," he said defensively. "I just been there more because my adopted niece, Connie, is livin' there."

Ozzie and Dunn were loading luggage when Puddles began to bark. Ozzie looked down the street and saw Nelda and Connie coming his way from the direction of the jail. Ozzie knew the girl had just told Layne Britton good-bye.

Puffing on a cigarillo, Cole Clinger watched Nelda approach. "Good morning, pretty lady," said Clinger, eyeing her hungrily.

"I'm in no mood for you," clipped Nelda. "Why don't you go crawl back under your rock?"

Clucking his tongue, the surly outlaw said, "Nelda, honey, that's no way to treat a fellow passenger."

"Passenger?" she gasped. "*You* are going on this stage?"

"Sure am, honey. I've got business in Dodge City."

"How did you know I was going to be a passenger?"

"Word gets around, my love," Clinger said, showing his yellow teeth. "I heard about Robert yesterday."

Ozzie Gisler stepped up to Cole Clinger and looked him square in the eye. With a raw edge in his voice, he said, "Let's get one thing straight, mister."

Clinger eyed him coldly, dropping the heel of his hand to the butt of the gun on his hip.

Without a pause or a flinch, Ozzie continued, "If you plan on ridin' this stage, you're gonna leave Nelda alone. And your dad-burned hand on that gun don't rattle my timbers one little bit. I'm the skipper of this ship, and you'll do as I say or *walk*. Understand?"

Clinger needed the stagecoach to carry out his plan. Removing his hand from the gun, he said, "Sorry, skipper. Didn't mean any harm."

"And another thing," breathed Ozzie heatedly, "Nelda ain't your 'honey.' A man ain't got no right callin' a woman by those endearin' names unless she gives him permission."

Nelda and Connie looked at each other, stunned and pleased at Ozzie's outburst. Clinger blinked and turned away without a word.

Nelda and Connie checked in with Harry Dunn and were introduced to Ted Drier and Hattie Weems.

"Okay, everybody," said Ozzie. "Time to roll!"

The passengers climbed aboard. The three women sat together in the forward seat with their backs to the driver, where the effects of the dust were less. Drier and Clinger occupied the opposite seat, the obese drummer taking up two thirds of the space. The passengers were feeling relief that none of them would have to ride on the uncomfortable seat in the middle.

While they waited for the driver and shotgunner to climb into the box, Drier talked incessantly. With a cold ball in her stomach, Nelda was thinking of Robert, while at the same time Ozzie's recent action warmed her heart. Connie was also experiencing mixed emotions. Her heart was heavy as she thought of Layne and the unjust prison sentence. Yet it fluttered with joy from the knowledge that at the end of this ride she would be reunited with her father.

Ozzie was about to climb up beside Bill in the box when Harry Dunn said, "You'll have to hold on a few minutes, Oz. I haven't told you yet, but you're going to have seven passengers."

"Who are the other two?"

"Tom Olson and Layne Britton. The deputy is escorting Layne to Fort Dodge."

"When'd this happen?" asked Ozzie with surprise. "I visited Layne in the jail yesterday, and he didn't know when he'd be goin' to Dodge."

"Templeton was waiting for me when I came to the office this morning. I couldn't tell you before without the other passengers overhearing. Thought it best they be already boarded when they found out they would be riding with a convicted criminal."

"Layne Britton ain't no criminal, and you know it," Ozzie said angrily.

"I know," agreed Dunn. "But being handcuffed to a lawman and taken to prison makes him look that way."

"The *real* criminal is still free," Ozzie said bitterly. "I wouldn't say his name, but his initials is *Dolph Catron*."

Looking down the street, Ozzie saw the two lawmen approaching with Layne Britton between them. Layne's wrists were shackled.

Ted Drier stopped jabbering when Cole Clinger peered through the window and said, "Looks like we got company."

"Layne!" exclaimed Connie, as he came up to the coach.

The tall man smiled at her and said, "Looks like we're going to take the trip together."

Ozzie opened the coach door. The bulky marshal leaned in and looked at the passengers. When he saw Cole Clinger, he uttered sullenly, "I hope you're leaving Wichita for good."

"You couldn't get that lucky," retaliated Clinger. "I'm going to Dodge on business. I'll be back."

Turning his attention to the others, Templeton said, "You folks'll be riding with a man who is on his way to prison at Fort Dodge. There's nothing to worry about. He's in handcuffs, and my deputy is going along."

Hattie Weems was instantly upset. Nelda turned to her and said, "Don't worry, dearie. This prisoner is harmless. Not only that, but he's innocent. He's going to prison on a trumped-up charge."

Disregarding her comment, Templeton continued, "Somebody's got to ride the middle seat. I want the prisoner right here next to the window so we can chain him to the doorpost."

Cole Clinger turned his dark, piercing eyes on the medicine drummer. "Looks like it'll have to be you, fat man. You take up two spaces."

Drier felt the power of Clinger's stare. Nodding his head, he grinned weakly and said, "Of course. I'll . . . ah . . . I'll be glad to ride the middle seat. I'm only going as far as Kingman, anyhow."

Layne Britton was placed opposite Connie, his wrists protruding through the windows and handcuffed around the doorpost. Cole Clinger was on the same seat at the other window, with Tom Olson in the middle. Next to Connie was Nelda. Tiny Hattie Weems sat opposite Cole Clinger.

Roy Templeton gave final instructions to his deputy through the door window and walked away. As Ozzie started to climb up to the box, Puddles yipped incessantly.

"Okay, you pesky, no good mutt," chuckled Ozzie, "let's see if Connie wants you."

Leaning through the window, dog in hands, Ozzie said, "Connie, this hound wants to see you."

The lovely brunette smiled, reaching for the dog. "I'll take her, Uncle Ozzie," she said, pulling Puddles inside.

"First rest stop she can come back to the box," said Ozzie.

"That'll be fine," agreed Connie, pulling the wiggly dog to her breast. Puddles began licking her under the chin, its stubby tail wagging full speed.

Cole Clinger looked around Ted Drier and flashed Connie a deceptive smile. He was not thinking about the affection she was getting from Puddles. He saw Connie as Charlie Prior's ticket out of Fort Dodge prison.

Up top, Ozzie Gisler snapped the reins and shouted, "Hee-yah!"

As the coach pulled away, Dolph Catron stood watching through the office window. His dark, sinister eyes gleamed as a grin pulled at the corners of his mouth. Everything had worked out perfectly. The deadline on the will was only about a month away. The Kellogg place would soon be his.

Dust lifted up under the Concord's wheels as it rolled onto Douglas Avenue. Young Danny Smith was sweeping the porch of the Sunflower Hotel. He paused to look at the coach and caught a glimpse of Layne Britton's solemn features in the window.

The team's hooves thundered hollowly on the bridge as the stagecoach crossed the lazy Arkansas River and headed westward.

Ted Drier spoke up and said, "If any of you folks are interested, I'm in patent medicine. Got just about anything to cure what ails you. Of course, I'm only supposed to sell wholesale to distributors, but I have some samples in my bags that I could let you have for a reasonable price." While the others did their best to ignore him, the drummer talked on.

Nelda thought of Robert. *Oh, God, let him live till I get there,* she prayed silently. *Please don't let my son die before I can see him.*

While Drier's monotonous chatter continued to fill the coach, Layne Britton studied the captivating face of the woman he adored. *Why am I so fortunate?* he asked himself. *A million men would give their right arms to have this lovely, sweet woman. And here she is willing to sacrifice herself and wait for me . . . cut another chunk out of her life, just as she did for her dying mother.*

Connie stroked the little dog in her lap and looked up at Layne. She smiled and silently mouthed the words, *I love you.* Layne's face beamed as he mouthed the same words in return.

Ted Drier's incessant chatter was getting on Nelda's nerves. When she had taken her fill, she butted in on him and said, "Mr. Drier, do you have medicine for sore ears?"

"Why, yes I do," he responded, not getting the point. "When we stop at the first station, I'll get you a bottle of our special eardrops from one of my bags in the boot. These eardrops are excellent for softening earwax, reducing swelling and inflammation of the ear canal, clearing up infection in the canal or on the drum itself. They stop earaches and prevent scaling, mastoids, abscesses, and boils. Our superlative eardrops contain an ingredient that comes from a plant that is grown in the Bahama Islands. They prevent hearing loss and have even been known to—"

"You didn't understand the lady's question, sir," cut in Tom Olson. "She is referring to the fact that your unending babble is making our ears sore. Why don't you just shut up and look at the lovely Kansas scenery?"

The fat man's jaw went slack. Eyes staring in disbelief at Olson's words, he said, "Well! That's a fine way for you, a public servant, to treat one of the public! I've a good mind to make contact with your superiors and see that you lose your job. And furthermore, I—"

Suddenly, Cole Clinger leaned forward and slammed his elbow savagely into Drier's middle. Breath whooshed from his mouth as he doubled over with pain.

"I ain't no public servant, fat man," lashed the outlaw, "so shut your trap or I'm gonna shut it for you!"

Hattie Weems blinked with shock.

The salesman's entire face sagged, while his eyes bulged. He stared at Cole Clinger's virulent features for a brief moment. Then, without a word, he twisted on the seat and glared out the window.

There were two relay stations between Wichita and Kingman. The cramped, dusty passengers were glad for both stops, which gave them an opportunity to stretch their legs. The sight of Kingman at sunset was even more welcome; here they would spend the night.

When the Concord wheeled to a halt in Kingman, Ted Drier quickly claimed his bags and disappeared without a word. The other passengers bid each other good night and went off to their sleeping quarters.

The next morning, Connie Lee awoke to a rush of emotions pulling at her heart. The dread was there when she thought of the man she loved going to prison. But joy was there, also, because after so many years of estrangement, she and her father were going to be reconciled.

A hearty breakfast was downed by crew and passengers, and by seven o'clock the big Concord was once again rumbling westward. Everyone was glad to be rid of the fat medicine drummer.

A relay station provided fresh horses some fifteen miles from Kingman, and Ozzie Gisler's stagecoach was once again on the move. At Pratt, Hattie Weems was greeted by her son, daughter-in-law, and three grandchildren. While the horses were being changed and the axles greased, Ozzie Gisler, Bill Henderson, and their five remaining passengers ate their midday meal.

The Kansas sun slid downward as the coach bore its occupants farther west. It was almost dark when it pulled into Greensburg, where it would lay over for the night. As the Concord ground to a halt, Ozzie set the brake and hollered downward, "Okay, folks, that's all for today! Dodge City tomorrow!"

For Deputy Tom Olson, the thought of Dodge City brought on a feeling of dread. He was increasingly convinced that Layne Britton had been framed. The man was plainly no murderer, and it didn't take much imagination to see Dolph Catron's motive for setting him up.

A dull, nauseous feeling crept over the deputy as he released Layne from the doorpost, waited for him to exit the coach, then rehandcuffed him: Olson was escorting an innocent man to prison.

During the evening meal at the way station, the deputy watched the melancholy faces of his prisoner and Connie Lee as they sat opposite each other at the table, and his heart went out to them. It was clear that they were in love. Connie's frequent visits to the jail and the way they looked at each other in the stagecoach left no doubt about it.

The deputy thought of the way Connie had laid her own interests aside during the past few years in order to make her mother's last days on earth as comfortable and happy as possible.

And now, he thought dismally, *Cora's gone. Connie finally had a chance to find happiness. She found it briefly in Layne Britton, only to lose it again.*

When the meal was over, Ozzie and his shotgunner went with the stationmaster to the barn to check on a section of harness that needed repairing. The stationmaster's wife and daughter began clearing the table, removing dirty dishes and leftover food to the kitchen.

Tom Olson had left the handcuffs on his prisoner during the meal. Shoving his chair back, he stood up and said, "Mr. Britton, would you and Miss Connie like some time together alone?"

Amazement showed on Layne Britton's finely chisled face. "Why, yes," he said, flicking a glance at Connie.

"The stagecoach is still sitting just outside the door," Olson said with a smile. "I'll chain you to the doorpost, and the two of you can have thirty minutes together in the coach."

Nelda Monroe, who was still seated, looked up and said, "Tom, may the angels sprinkle stardust all over you for that!"

"Thank you, Tom," Connie said, smiling amiably.

Layne rose from the table and stood full height. Looking down at the deputy, he spoke with appreciation. "That may be the last we'll be alone together for a long time. Thank you."

Nelda watched Connie and the two men go through the door. When it closed, she half whispered, "Bless that deputy." As she rose from her chair, she suddenly realized that she and Cole Clinger were the only ones left in the dining hall. The outlaw was rounding the long table and coming toward her.

Nelda stiffened. "Forget it, Cole," she said, frost in her words. "Don't you touch me!"

Clinger halted, just out of reach. "I don't need any more belts across the face, honey," he said, palms forward. "Couldn't you spare a man a little kiss or two?"

"When I see a man," she retorted, "I'll give it some consideration."

A sneer formed on Clinger's lips. "Too good for me, huh?"

"I never said that, Cole," Nelda replied, shaking her head. "You're just not my type, okay? Now leave me be. I've got a son dying, or maybe already dead, at Fort Dodge. No more talk." With that, she moved swiftly across the room and passed into a dark hallway that led to the sleeping quarters.

Outside, Tom Olson fished in his vest pocket for the small key. The moon had risen, spraying the prairie with silver light. Connie entered the coach, and Layne followed and sat beside her. Tom unlocked one cuff. Layne extended his hands through the windows, with the doorpost between. The deputy clamped the cuff on the free wrist, but before he squeezed it shut, he shook his head and said, "This is stupid. If I do it like this, you can't put your arms around her." Leaning inside, he put Layne's hands together and cuffed them.

"Much obliged," grinned Layne.

"I'll be sitting over here on the porch," said Olson. "See you in half an hour."

As the deputy's footsteps died away, the tall man looped his shackled hands over Connie's head and pulled her close. Each could see the other's eyes by the moon's pale radiance.

Connie's lips were like velvet as Layne kissed her tenderly. "I love you," he said softly, his breath warm on her face.

As she repeated the words, Layne kissed her again, this time soundly. Then he leaned back and for a long, silent moment studied her face.

"What are you doing?" she whispered.

"Memorizing the look in your eyes. I want to be able to remember it clearly when we're apart."

Connie lifted her face and kissed him as tears surfaced in her eyes. Placing her head against his chest, she whispered, "Oh, Layne, darling, I—"

"Ssssh!" he breathed. "Don't talk, honey. Just let me hold you. This has to last for a long time."

Silent tears scalded Connie's cheeks as Layne held her nearly breathless in the warmth of his powerful arms.

It seemed only a brief moment had passed when Tom Olson came to say that the half hour was over.

Chapter Thirteen

Morning brought sunshine to the rolling plains, but not to the hearts of Connie Lee and Layne Britton. Today they would reach their destination. The shadow of vertical bars would darken their lives before the sun touched the western horizon.

The dusty Concord rolled out of Greensburg at seven o'clock. There were two way stations between Greensburg and Dodge City. They arrived at the first one by nine-thirty. At nine-fifty, the station was falling behind in a swirling cloud of dust.

The coach reached the last relay station at noon, and the weary travelers disembarked and headed inside for lunch. Afterward, they would ride another three hours, ending their journey at approximately three-thirty.

Deputy Olson held Layne Britton outside alone while the last of the passengers disappeared inside. "Look, Mr. Britton," the young man said, "this thing is eating up my insides."

"What's that?" asked Layne.

"I want to ask you a question man to man."

"Shoot."

Looking the ex-gunfighter square in the eye, he said, "Did you gun down Boone Foss?"

"No, I didn't," replied Layne, holding his gaze steady.

Olson paused, then said, "I believe you." Looking around to make sure no one was listening, he said with lowered voice, "The key to the handcuffs is in the left pocket of my vest. Punch me a hard one. Be sure it leaves a mark. When I go down, take the key and run. I noticed a saddled horse standing beside the barn. Get on it and ride."

"Listen," said Layne, "I can't—"

"All I can lose is my job," cut in Olson hastily. "I can't stand it, knowing you're going to prison innocent and I'm taking you there. Hurry up. Clip me a good one and go!"

"Tom, I appreciate what you're willing to do," said Layne with sincerity, "but it wouldn't be any good. I'd be running the rest of my life."

"Not if you were free to find a flaw in Dolph Catron's armor."

"Be hard to do that while hiding," Layne said glumly. "It's best that I go on and serve the five years. Then I can live without looking over my shoulder."

"Okay," nodded Olson, with regret.

"Listen, Tom," said the tall man, looking deep into the deputy's eyes, "I'll never forget what you just offered to do. Never."

After lunch, the Concord's occupants settled into their seats for the final stretch. Cole Clinger felt the exhilaration of knowing Charlie Prior would be a free man shortly. Nelda Monroe found herself praying again. Somehow Robert had to live long enough for her to see him. Layne and Connie looked at each other wistfully.

The stagecoach rolled on. At three-fifteen Ozzie Gisler shouted from up top, "Dodge City, straight ahead!"

Cole Clinger grew tense. The heavy stand of trees where his men were waiting would come into view any second. Suddenly, there it was. He hoped nothing had detained his gang. He had to make his move *now*. He leaned out the window to see if there were any other vehicles or riders on the road. Peering through the dust was difficult, but it looked clear both ways.

Whipping the gun from his holster, Clinger dogged back the hammer and put the muzzle to Tom Olson's head in one smooth motion. Suddenly all eyes were on the outlaw. "Tell Gisler to pull off the road and stop!" he barked.

Olson hesitated. In anger, Cole pressed the muzzle hard to the deputy's head and snapped, "Do it now, or I'll splatter your brains all over these nice people!"

As Olson obeyed, Clinger seized the lawman's gun and jammed it under his own belt.

Ozzie responded to Olson's command, veered off the road, and hauled the vehicle to a stop. Inside the coach, Clinger said, "Now tell the shotgunner to throw his twelve-gauge on the ground."

"Clinger's got a gun to my head, Ozzie!" hollered Olson. "Tell Bill to toss the shotgun to the dirt!"

"What are you pulling, Cole?" demanded Nelda.

At the same instant the shotgun clattered to the ground, the thundering hooves of a dozen horses came out of the deep shadows from the small forest nearby. Smiling at the sound, Clinger ignored Nelda's question and looked out the window.

Lefty Scofield, with gun drawn, rode close and said, "Right on schedule, boss."

"Let's keep it that way," responded Clinger. "Tell that old fool in the box to drive this thing into the trees."

Looking up at the driver, Lefty bellowed, "Hey you! Take the coach up there into the trees. All the way in, so it can't be seen from the road."

"What's goin' on?" challenged Ozzie.

"Don't ask questions," rasped Lefty. "Just do as you're told or we'll start shooting! First bird to go off the roost will be you!"

Reluctantly, Ozzie spoke to his team and drove them deep into the trees. As he brought the Concord to a halt in a clearing and set the brake, Clinger's men pressed around it, slipping from their saddles.

Cole Clinger backed out of the stagecoach, gun leveled on Olson. "Okay, Deputy, you and Nelda get out."

When Nelda moved forward in the seat, she momentarily blocked the deputy from Clinger's view. Taking advantage of the opportunity, Olson reached in his vest pocket and then pressed the small key into Connie's palm. She quickly closed her fingers around it.

Connie looked at Layne fearfully as Nelda and Olson moved into the sun-dappled shade of the tall trees. "What are they doing?" she asked tremulously.

"I don't know," responded Layne. "Whatever it is, they're up to no good."

At that instant, Clinger stuck his head inside and said, "I want you over here, honey." He was directing Connie to slide across the seat, putting her in the opposite corner from Layne. When she had done so, Clinger said, "You stay right there."

Layne threw him a hot glare. "What are you up to, Cole?"

Clinger's only answer was, "You could have thrown in with me, Layne. Now it's too late. You go on and rot in that stinking prison." Turning toward his circle of gunmen, he called out, "Leon! Get over here."

Leon Pelton showed his friends a toothy smile as he moved toward the stagecoach. He was going to be in the coach with the beautiful woman while they stayed outside.

Connie's face paled and tightened as the foul-smelling outlaw climbed in and sat opposite her on the same seat as Layne Britton. She did not like the lustful look in his deep-set, sinister eyes.

A wicked grin curled Leon's mouth. "I'm gonna be your watchdog, sweetheart," he said, "until this ordeal is over."

"She's not your sweetheart!" Layne rasped. "And what are you talking about? What's going on?"

"You'll find out soon enough, big man," sneered the outlaw. "And I'll call this beautiful doll anything I want to, you hear me?" Leering at Connie, he said, "Might just get me a sweet little kiss."

Anger boiled up in Layne Britton. With voice as brittle as winter ice, he said, "My hands may be shackled, but my feet aren't. You touch her and I'll kick you all the way to hell!"

Leon unsheathed his revolver, cocked it, and swung

the muzzle on Layne. "Can you kick through a .44 slug, big man?"

Cole Clinger's voice came through the coach's open door, pungent and stern. "You stay away from that woman, Leon! All you're in there for is to see she don't escape!"

"Don't worry, boss," he replied, easing down the hammer and holstering the weapon. "I wouldn't think of letting this beautiful hunk of womanhood get away."

Connie knew she must get the key into Layne's hands. Leaping cornerwise across the coach, she screamed, "I'm not staying in here!"

Leon lunged for her. Pretending to claw at the doorpost, Connie slipped the key into Layne's hand.

Careful not to hurt her, Leon forced Connie back to her place. Easing down on the seat facing her, he said gruffly, "No more of that kind of stuff, honey."

Outside, Cole Clinger now had Nelda Monroe, Tom Olson, Bill Henderson, and Ozzie Gisler sitting on the ground next to the stagecoach. Puddles lay next to Ozzie, sensing that things were askew.

Clinger positioned himself where he could address the prisoners both inside and outside the stagecoach. "Now here's the story. Miss Lee, here in the coach, is the daughter of Colonel Morgan Lee, commandant at Fort Dodge, where my friend, Charlie Prior, is locked up on a life sentence. I mean to get him out. Anybody here tries to stop me, I'll kill him!"

After pausing for effect, Clinger continued, "The colonel's going to get a note from his daughter, written by her own hand. It will say that we have her and five other hostages. Lee is to send Charlie out with Lefty, who will deliver the note. If the two of them are not back before sundown, Connie is first to die! Everyone, including Connie, will be released only if the colonel complies and there is no interference by the army."

Inside the stagecoach, Connie looked fearfully at Layne.

"Do as he tells you," Layne said firmly.

Connie wrote the note with pencil and paper supplied by the outlaws. It was dictated word for word by Cole Clinger.

It was just after four o'clock when Lefty Scofield lifted his sombrero to the top of his head and tightened the neck cord. Placing the folded note in a pocket of his Mexican-style jacket, he mounted up and galloped away.

Nelda Monroe was becoming frantic with worry. Every minute she was held here, the chances of seeing her son alive grew slimmer. She rose to her feet and took a deep breath. Approaching Clinger, who stood watching horse and rider fade into the distance, she said with a tremor in her voice, "Cole, you mustn't hold me here. Robert may still be alive. I must go to him."

Clinger regarded the woman with cold, hard eyes. His voice was like acid as he said in a hissing undertone, "You lost your chance to be in my good graces. Now go back and sit by your boyfriend."

"Cole," she pleaded. "You can't do this! My son is dying!"

"Everybody dies, Nelda," the outlaw sneered.

Ozzie Gisler felt his skin crawl at the treatment Nelda was getting from Clinger. He leaped to his feet in anger. Frank Miller, standing nearby, drew and cocked his gun. The dry sound of clicking metal met the old man's ears. He checked himself as Miller said in an ominous tone, "Sit down, Gisler, or I'll drop you in your tracks!"

Ozzie scorched the man's craggy face with burning eyes for a long moment. Swinging the same hot glare on Clinger, he said, "It ain't gonna hurt nothin' to let her go to the fort! You still got enough hostages here!"

"You get on the ground and shut your trap!" retaliated the outlaw leader, pointing a stiff finger at Ozzie.

Miller stepped forward and pressed the muzzle of his revolver against Ozzie's temple. "Sit down!"

Puddles bared her teeth and growled at the hostile man. As Ozzie lowered himself to the ground, he spoke softly to his dog, quieting her.

Layne Britton looked on helplessly, anger coursing through his veins, as Nelda screamed, "Cole! You've got to let me go!" Her body was trembling in spasms of fear and panic.

Without warning, Cole Clinger slapped her hard with

his open hand. "You ain't going nowhere! You could have been my woman, but you were too proud. Now, it's just too bad!"

While Nelda reeled from the blow, Ozzie Gisler sprang upward, blind with rage. Darting ahead of him, Puddles attacked Cole Clinger's pant leg with a vicious growl. The gang reacted, swinging their guns on the charging stage driver, but Ozzie was on Clinger so fast there was no way to shoot without hitting their boss.

The stage driver collided with Clinger like a battering ram. The two men rolled on the ground, fists flying. Puddles was growling and snapping at the outlaw, rolling in the dust amid the flailing arms and legs. At one point, the little dog was thrown free of the battle. Art Winkler moved in and kicked her violently with his booted foot. Puddles yelped and dashed under the stagecoach, sucking hard for air.

Frank Miller stepped up beside Art Winkler, attempting to get a clear shot at Ozzie. Winkler touched his arm, saying, "Let the boss handle him."

At that moment, the two combatants found their feet, breathing hard. Clinger swung a wild punch and missed. The wiry stagecoach driver caught him solid on the jaw, and the outlaw dropped like a chopped tree.

"Look out, Ozzie!" shouted Nelda, seeing that Frank Miller was aiming his gun at him.

Before Miller had a chance to fire, Art Winkler stepped in and clubbed the stage driver with his gun barrel. Ozzie slumped to the ground, unconscious.

Layne Britton watched it all. He was nearly beside himself, wanting to do something. Up to this point, he had found no opportunity to use the key—Leon Pelton was too close. Layne would have to bide his time.

At the fort, Lefty Scofield stood in Colonel Morgan Lee's office as the commandant read Connie's note. The square-shouldered colonel raised his eyes from the paper and looked at the cocky, insolent features of Cole Clinger's right-hand man. Morgan had been living for the moment he would see his daughter, anticipating the joy of holding her in his arms. And now these outlaws not only had robbed him of the joy but were threatening her life. Morgan Lee caged his burning fury, thinking of Connie's safety.

Scorning the colonel with a defiant look, Lefty flipped the sombrero to his back and said, "Let's have Charlie, Colonel, or you've got a dead daughter."

Morgan's heart pounded like a hammer. Charlie Prior was working on a chain gang several miles north of Fort Dodge. The gang was not due back until dark. To make it back before sundown, prisoner and guard would have to ride like the wind.

Acting quickly, the colonel moved for the door. Lefty blocked his way. "Where you going?" he demanded.

"Prior isn't here," retorted Morgan. "I'll send a rider after him. Then I'll explain it."

Lefty stepped aside, watching and listening as the colonel gave hasty instructions to his secretary. The young corporal bounded out the door instantly.

Returning to the office, Morgan explained the situation, and the outlaw said curtly, "I'll wait, Colonel. But me and Charlie had better be with my boss before sundown."

The colonel went to his desk and sat down, still holding his anger in check. Lefty stood with his back to Morgan, watching men move about on the parade ground. Silently, Morgan Lee studied the outlaw's broad back. Measuring him mentally, he realized the two of them were close to the same size and built much alike. A plan of action began to form in his mind.

Morgan doubted that Connie would be released, even if the outlaws got Charlie Prior. There was only one way to foil the whole thing. Circling the desk, the muscular colonel moved toward Lefty. Without fear or caution, Lefty began to turn to meet him. Moving with the swiftness of a cat, Morgan released his fury, scissored Scofield's neck in the crook of his right arm while seizing his wrist with his left hand. He threw the surprised outlaw over his hip, slamming him savagely to the floor.

Lefty let out a cry as the angry colonel pinned him down and yanked the hammerlocked arm upward.

"Where's the stagecoach?" hissed Morgan.

At Lefty's silence, the powerful colonel rammed the arm upward. Letting out a yell, the outlaw sucked air through his teeth and said, "I'll tell! I'll tell!"

Morgan Lee held him there until he was satisfied the man had given him the proper location of the coach. Suddenly there was a rapid knock at the door, then Corporal Stram and three soldiers burst through without waiting for an answer.

"Colonel, are you all right?" asked Stram.

"Just fine," breathed Morgan, releasing his ironlike hold. "Help me get this man's clothes off."

An hour later, with Lefty Scofield locked up, Colonel Morgan Lee paced the floor of his office, wearing the outlaw's pants, gun, and Mexican jacket. The sombrero dangled on his broad back by the neck cord.

Morgan had dispatched a squad of cavalrymen to the area where Cole Clinger and his men held their hostages. They were to lay back to the north, out of sight behind some low bluffs until Morgan appeared on horseback with Charlie Prior and had entered the stand of trees.

While pacing, the colonel peered through his window and saw a body being carried from the hospital, a sheet pulled up over the face. Opening his office door, Morgan said, "Corporal, go find out who just died."

Impatiently, the colonel returned to his office window. The shadows were lengthening. The deadline was drawing near.

Chapter Fourteen

Cole Clinger was doing his own pacing as the sun lowered toward the earth's western rim. Over two hours had passed. Lefty should have been back with Charlie Prior long before now. What was holding them? The outlaw rubbed his sore jaw and silently cursed Ozzie Gisler. The stage driver was more man than Clinger had counted on.

Layne had found it impossible to use the key on his handcuffs with Leon Pelton sitting next to him. He would get only one chance. He dare not try it until the odds of success were at least half in his favor.

Connie thought hard on how to divert Leon's attention from Layne without alerting the outlaws outside.

Nelda Monroe sat on the ground next to Ozzie, holding a wet cloth to the swollen gash on his head. She was desperate. She had to do something. As Cole Clinger paced in front of them, her eyes fell on the handle of the revolver in his holster. Each time he passed to the right, it was within reach.

The determined woman let the gun pass her twice more. The third time, she lunged for it. The tense outlaw saw the movement from the corner of his eye. Just as Nelda's fingers closed on the grips, he pivoted, seizing her wrist. Throwing his weight back, Clinger jerked the woman to her feet. When Nelda reached full height, he sank his fingers into the thick hair of her head. Jerking her head backward with a violent snap, he yanked her toward him. Tripping her with an outstretched foot, he sent her sprawling in the dirt.

Ozzie Gisler's attempt to get up was met with Frank Miller's gun pointing between his eyes.

Enraged, Layne Britton bellowed, "Clinger! You've got no cause to manhandle her like that! Do that again, and I'll tear this stage apart and come after you!"

"Leon!" yelled Clinger, standing over the disheveled Nelda. "If Britton makes another outburst, shoot him!"

"With pleasure, boss!" Leon called back.

Colonel Morgan Lee was relieved when he saw the two riders swing through the gate and head for his house. Charlie Prior was ushered quickly into Morgan's office, his prison grays stained with sweat.

"What's this all about, Colonel?" asked Prior. "What're you doing in that getup?"

Morgan Lee eyed the slender, dark-complexioned man and said, "Charlie, I've got a serious problem."

While the convict listened, the colonel filled him in on the events of the day. Quickly, he explained the details of his plan to thwart Cole Clinger's scheme.

"Now," concluded Morgan, running splayed fingers through his heavy shock of silver hair, "you may feel indebted to Clinger for trying to break you out of here. But believe me, he's not going to get away with it. If you will do what I ask, we might pull this off without bloodshed. If you don't, I'm leading my men in there like killing snakes. Clinger and his gang will all die, and you're still in prison for life." Morgan Lee had stretched the truth about going in like killing snakes. An all-out attack could get Connie and the other hostages killed. But he needed Charlie Prior, so the man had to believe that his hopes for escape were futile.

"Is that all that's in it for me?" asked Prior. "Just to know I helped stop bloodshed?"

"No, that's not all," said Morgan, ready to play his trump card. "If you will play along, I'll do my dead-level best to get your sentence reduced."

"Your dead-level best?" said Prior, warily.

"I'm not the civil law in Kansas," responded Morgan, "but in my position, I do have influence. You have my word. I will do my utmost to get your sentence shortened considerably. It's a better deal than you're going to get siding with Clinger."

"I'll do it," replied Prior without hesitation.

The lower rim of the sun was resting on the horizon as the two men rode out of the fort, Colonel Lee on Lefty Scofield's horse and Prior on an army mount.

An exasperated Cole Clinger eyed the sun through the tall trees. Only the top half of it was visible now. The whole thing would be gone in a few minutes.

Clinger had a lookout man stationed at the west edge of the small forest. Suddenly the man caught sight of two riders coming toward them in the orange light of the setting sun. "Hey, boss!" he shouted. "Come here!"

Leaving the clearing, Clinger threaded his way through the tall timber. Reaching the edge, he followed the man's finger with his eyes. Squinting, he said excitedly, "It's Charlie and Lefty! We did it."

Clinger's old outlaw pal was waving, and he waved back. The riders were coming at a full gallop, and Clinger pointed them to the opening where the stagecoach had found its way through the trees. Then he ran back to the clearing, the lookout man on his heels.

Seconds later, the two riders rode into the clearing to the cheers of the gang members. All eyes were on Charlie Prior, who was smiling broadly. Morgan Lee wore Scofield's sombrero pulled low. He turned his face toward the horse as he slid groundward.

As Prior's feet touched earth, Clinger hurried toward him, saying with elation, "Charlie! Good to see you! Hey, Lefty! You deserve a medal! You—"

Suddenly the colonel pulled Charlie Prior to him and held a gun to his head, hammer cocked. "Hold it right there, Clinger!" came Morgan's thunderous voice.

Ozzie Gisler's head came up. "Morgan Lee!" he exclaimed.

Inside the coach, Connie and Layne whipped their heads around. At the same instant, Leon Pelton drew his revolver, pulled back the hammer, and pointed it at Connie's heart.

Cole Clinger stood frozen in his tracks, eyes wide. Morgan shook the sombrero from his head as Leon shouted from the coach, "Tell him to let Charlie go and put down the gun, Cole! I've got my gun on his daughter!"

Holding Charlie Prior firmly, Morgan Lee said fiercely, "Tell your man in the coach to put down *his* gun, Clinger! Tell him to come out of the stagecoach *now!*"

Cole Clinger burst into laughter. "Maybe I ought to remind you, Colonel, that's your *daughter* he has in there. Charlie is only my *friend.*"

"Tell *all* your men to drop their guns!" commanded Morgan.

Clinger laughed again and started to speak when suddenly a dozen rifles were heard being cocked from the deep shadows of the surrounding trees. Clinger's mouth sagged. His eyes widened. The outlaws stood frozen like statues, while the hostages looked on with apprehension. Leon Pelton threw a worried glance out the window.

Morgan Lee's voice was like the cutting edge of a ripsaw. "If your man hurts my daughter, Clinger, my men will drop you and every one of your gang in your tracks!"

Clinger threw back a challenge. "You'd never give such a command, Colonel!"

"I've already given it!"

"Are you willing to let your daughter die to prove it?"

"Are you willing to die to find out?"

"Well, now," said Clinger insolently, "looks like we've got us a standoff here."

Inside the stagecoach, Connie knew the whole situation hinged on her precarious position. She looked at Leon Pelton, who was still seated across from her, leveling the weapon on her heart. The woman's nerves were strung tight, but the sound of her father's voice and the confidence that Layne could handle Leon if his hands were free gave her courage.

Forcing strength into her voice, Connie said, "Can you really pull that trigger, Leon? Can you actually shoot me in cold blood?"

Beaded moisture formed on the outlaw's brow.

"Are you going to do it, if Cole gives the command?" pressed Connie, her heart thundering. "My father is a man of his word. He means what he says. Your whole gang will go down. *You* especially, Leon, if you shoot me." Layne Britton knew exactly what the woman was doing. While she held Leon's undivided attention, he twisted a wrist and inserted the tiny key in its slot.

Leon Pelton blinked in uncertainty. The muzzle of his revolver was still lined on the woman's breast.

Connie squeezed him further. "What do you owe Cole Clinger, Leon? Do you owe him your life?"

As Leon ran a shaky palm over his sweaty face, Connie flicked a glance to Layne. With his steel-gray eyes, he told her to throw herself low, across the seat. As Connie instantly reacted, Layne moved with the swiftness of a cougar. He clamped both hands on Leon's wrist and swung the muzzle upward.

Suddenly the gun went off. Outside, every man's eyes shifted to the stagecoach. Morgan Lee's body jerked as the revolver in Leon Pelton's hand discharged. He did not see that the bullet tore through the roof. Then, as the coach rocked, it became evident that Layne Britton was loose and the two men were in a struggle.

With superior strength, Layne twisted the gun from the outlaw's hands. Leon loosed a violent oath just as Layne cracked him savagely with the gun barrel. He slumped to the floor in a stone-cold heap. Connie's eyes were wide, her face ashen.

"Colonel Lee!" Layne hollered through the window. "Danger's over in here! Connie's safe!" Layne enfolded Connie's trembling body in his arms as tears of relief filled his eyes.

Outside the coach, Frank Miller's impetuous nature took over. Pivoting, he swung his gun on the colonel, who still held Charlie Prior. Reacting instinctively to Miller's move, Art Winkler lifted his own weapon. Like an instant clap of thunder, several rifles roared. Winkler and Miller went down dead in a hail of bullets.

Clinger's remaining men dropped their guns, as if the weapons had suddenly turned red-hot, and thrust their hands skyward. A bit slower and more reluctantly, Clinger did the same.

Blue uniforms suddenly swarmed the place, corralling the outlaws. The silver-haired Morgan Lee released a timorous Charlie Prior to his soldiers, holstered the gun, and swung his yearning gaze to the stagecoach. Layne Britton was helping Connie from the vehicle when the eyes of father and daughter met in the light of the setting sun.

Layne let go of Connie's hand as she moved with a dazed expression toward the man she had not seen in six years. Morgan took slow, calculated steps toward his beautiful daughter, his eyes glistening. Father and daughter paused within one step of each other, their tear-filled eyes locked in wonderment.

Connie took a quick breath as a tiny smile touched her lips. "Hello, Daddy," she said softly.

"Hello, darling," breathed her father, opening his arms.

Morgan Lee enfolded his daughter and held her tight as they both wept unashamedly for a long moment. Tenderly they kissed each other's cheeks. Then the colonel held her at arm's length and looked her up and down. "What a beautiful woman you've turned out to be!" he exclaimed.

Blushing, Connie dipped her chin, saying demurely, "Oh, Daddy."

Nelda waited as long as she could while father and daughter had a few tender words together. Then she approached Fort Dodge's commandant. Connie saw her coming and said, "Daddy, I want you to meet my very dear friend, Nelda Monroe."

After greeting each other, Nelda said, "Colonel, my son, Robert, is in your prison. I received word from your chief surgeon that he had been critically wounded in some kind of scuffle and might not live long. He said I should come as soon as possible. Do you happen to know—"

The grave, weighty look that formed on Morgan Lee's features gave Nelda her answer. A cold wave of anguish was already washing over her before he said solemnly, "Your son died just moments before I left the fort, Mrs. Monroe. I'm sorry."

The effect of Morgan's words came to Nelda slowly. As they registered, she said with a thick tongue, "Are you telling me that Robert was alive at the time I should have arrived at the fort?"

"Yes, ma'am," nodded the colonel. "He died less than an hour ago."

Suddenly the woman's face was alive with a deep-crimson flush that went all the way to her eyes. Burning wrath ignited the bed of sorrow in Nelda's heart, turning it to uncontrollable passion. A branching vein stood out in the center of her forehead as she looked at Cole Clinger, who stood less than ten feet away beside a man in blue uniform. Her anger exploded. "Damn you, Clinger! You kept me from being with my boy when he died!"

The colonel stepped in front of Nelda as he ordered the soldier who held Clinger's arm to get him out of sight.

Nelda looked at the butt of the gun on Morgan Lee's hip. Instantly she snatched it from the holster, thumbed back the hammer, and swung the muzzle on Clinger. The Colt .44 boomed.

Morgan tried to grab her, but she sidestepped him and rushed at Clinger, who lay on the ground, a bullet in his shoulder. As the blue smoke lifted, the angry woman stood over the bleeding outlaw, holding the weapon with both hands. The hammer was back, and the black, ominous muzzle was lined between his eyes. Nelda's hands quivered with fury.

One of the soldiers took a step toward her from behind. "No!" shouted the colonel. "If you touch her, Clinger's a dead man!" The soldier halted and stepped back.

With eyes of seething hatred, Nelda glared at the wounded outlaw. Clinger, teeth clenched in pain, stared with rising horror at the woman's face and the quivering, dark muzzle.

"My son died today, Clinger," Nelda murmured tartly, lips pulled thin. "What was it you said? *Everybody dies.* Yes, even the mighty Cole Clinger. Well, this is your day, too, you dirty—"

"Mrs. Monroe!" cut in Morgan Lee. "Don't do it!"

Nelda's finger was on the trigger. The fallen outlaw's pallid face glistened with sweat.

"It will be murder, Mrs. Monroe," spoke the colonel with a calm voice. "As it stands now, I can promise you there will be no arrest . . . no prosecution. We'll just forget what happened."

"Clinger won't forget it!" she snapped.

"Y-yes I w-will, Nelda," gulped the outlaw. "R-right here in f-front of all these witnesses, I p-promise. I'll never bother you."

"I'd rather you rotted in hell!" she retorted, gripping the quivering gun hard.

"Nelda, darlin', listen to me." It was the gentle voice of Ozzie Gisler as he came up close from behind. Circling slowly, the stage driver moved to where she could see him from the corner of her eye.

Without moving her line of sight from Clinger's frightened face, she said through her teeth, "I'm gonna kill him, Ozzie."

"Honey, listen," he said with care, "you'll go to prison for murder if you do. He ain't worth it."

"He deserves to die!" she argued. "It would give me great pleasure to splatter what brains he's got all over Kansas." Sucking in a shaky breath, she said, "Besides, I haven't got that much to live for."

Connie watched Ozzie's face as he said, "Well, what about me?"

"What do you mean?" asked Nelda, keeping her eyes and the deadly weapon on the bridge of Cole Clinger's nose.

"I mean, I love you, that's what."

The terrified outlaw observed a slight change in Nelda's visage. Some of the fire left her eyes, and the hard features softened.

Connie's hand went to her mouth at Ozzie's words, her eyes wide in a mixture of disbelief and pleasure.

Without moving, Nelda said, "Ozzie, do you mean that? Or are you just trying to placate me into letting this human scum go to prison?"

"I'm s-sure he m-means it, Nelda," spoke up the bleeding outlaw.

"You shut up!" she railed at Clinger. "Let him do his own talking."

"Yes, I mean it!" exclaimed Ozzie. "It's been comin' on for some time, now. I've just been hidin' from it. Didn't you see how mad I got at this stinkin' skunk when he manhandled you?"

"It wasn't just because I'm a woman?"

"No, darlin'," Ozzie assured her. "I really do love you. Besides, it'd be mighty hard for you and me to get married if you were behind bars!"

Still holding steady, Nelda asked, "Is that a proposal?"

"That's what I'd call it, honey," Ozzie said, tilting his head. "I ain't never made one before, but that sure enough is what it is!"

Slowly, Nelda Monroe let her arms relax. Cole Clinger laid his head back with a sigh of relief.

Tearfully, Nelda relinquished the gun to Morgan Lee as Ozzie Gisler took her into his arms.

Chapter Fifteen

Connie Lee remained at Fort Dodge for a week, visiting with her father and Layne Britton while she awaited Ozzie Gisler's next run to Wichita. The cavalry troops enjoyed Connie's visit almost as much as she did. Her singular beauty and womanly poise were the talk of the fort.

Twice daily Morgan Lee escorted his daughter across the sun-bleached grounds to the prison, where she talked with Layne through an exterior barred window. During that time Colonel Lee learned the full story of Layne's conviction and came to like and admire the man.

On one occasion, as father and daughter walked away from the prison building, he looked down into her wistful eyes. Putting an arm around her shoulders, he said, "You really do love that young man, don't you?"

"With all my heart, Daddy," she answered softly.

"You really figure he's worth five years of waiting?"

Looking up into the green eyes that matched her own, she said, "I would wait an entire lifetime for him."

As they strolled, the colonel grew pensive. After several moments, Connie asked, "What are you thinking about?"

The square-shouldered man took a deep breath and let it out slowly. "I was just wishing your mother had loved me as much as you love Layne. If she had, no Dolph Catron could have taken her away from me."

Connie's stomach felt a tinge of nausea at the sound

of the repugnant name. As this feeling passed, a cold ball of bitterness took its place. "That vile beast has taken a lot away from both of us," she said with a raw edge to her voice. "If it weren't for him, we'd have had our happy home, and you and I wouldn't have lost six years of our lives together. Now he has taken five years away from Layne and me."

Morgan Lee tightened the arm he had around Connie's shoulders as she choked up with emotion. "Life has a lot of mysteries, honey," he said levelly, "but the Good Book says a man eventually reaps what he sows. You can count on that."

On the last evening before her departure, father and daughter finished their meal in the dining room of his big house. As they rose from the table, the handsome, silver-haired man said, "Honey, I'd like to talk to you. Let's go out on the front porch." He guided Connie toward the door, saying, "These days have passed all too quickly."

"Yes, they have," she agreed.

On the porch, the two settled in wicker chairs and took a long look at the dying light that clung to the western horizon.

Approaching the subject he had in mind, the colonel looked at his daughter through the gathering gloom and said, "Connie, why don't you let me send for all your things, and you just move in here? The room you are staying in can be yours."

"That's sweet of you, Daddy," she said warmly, "but I couldn't do that."

"Why not?"

"I'm going on twenty-one," Connie explained. "It would be different if I were a child. I should be out on my own."

"But if you lived here, you could see Layne every day."

"That would be wonderful, Daddy," she conceded, "but I must stay in Wichita for Layne's sake, too. I have a job there. I can put money aside for us while he's in prison. Layne has lost the ranch, so he won't have anything when he gets out."

"I admire you for that," her father said, "but I have a substantial amount saved up. You and Layne can have it. I—"

"No," the woman replied sternly. "We would not take it. We must make our own way."

"But where are you going to live when Nelda marries Ozzie?" he asked in concern.

"Nelda told me before she left that since Uncle Ozzie's house is smaller, they're going to live in hers. They had talked it over. I can live in his house and pay my rent by helping Nelda with her sewing when she gets behind."

"Well, honey," said Morgan Lee, sighing audibly. "I guess you've got things taken care of."

"Don't worry, Daddy, you won't be rid of me completely," the vivacious woman said, laughing lightly. "I'll be back to visit as often as Weneke's General Store can spare me!"

The seventh morning came all too soon for Connie. She loved only three men in the world, and today she would leave two of them behind. The third would be the man to crack the whip over the horses' heads and take her away. The leather-faced old driver had wired to say he would come to the fort to pick up Connie after departing Dodge City.

Layne was brought from the prison to the colonel's quarters some thirty minutes before Ozzie's stagecoach was due. Connie was waiting alone in her father's office when Corporal Stram opened the door, allowed the tall man to pass through, and then closed it.

Layne stood for a moment in his prison grays, drinking in her delicate beauty with his eyes. "The Lord must be mighty proud of Himself," he said with conviction.

Puzzlement captured the woman's features. "Why?"

"For making someone as beautiful and wonderful as you!"

Crimson slowly crept up her face. "Layne Britton," she breathed, "I love you."

"It's killing me to let you go," he said with difficulty.

Taking her slender frame in his arms, Layne kissed her passionately.

"Five years will pass in no time," Connie breathed.

"Four years and fifty-one weeks," said Layne, forcing a note of optimism into his voice. "Then I'll be free, and you will become Mrs. Layne Britton. We will have the rest of our lives together."

"Then let's agree," Connie said thoughtfully, "that time is a stranger to us. As far as we are concerned, we are not in its possession. Our lives will not really begin until the day you are free and we are together!"

"So be it."

Time disappeared as they stood holding and kissing each other. But all too soon their dream was shattered by the sound of thumping hooves, spinning wheels, and rattling harnesses.

"Miss Connie!" called the corporal through the closed door. "The stagecoach is here!"

Folding her to him, Layne kissed Connie passionately, until the breath was nearly gone out of her. "I love you, Connie," he said, his heart pounding.

"And I love you, Layne," she responded.

The sorrowful young couple stepped out into the brilliant sunlight. Morgan Lee was chatting with Ozzie Gisler, who was seated up in the box.

"Hello, beautiful!" came the old man's customary greeting.

"Hello, handsome," came the woman's gentle reply.

Ozzie turned to Layne. "Howdy, son!"

"Nice to see you, Oz," said Layne.

Reluctantly, Ozzie said to Connie, "We gotta get goin', honey." He picked up Puddles, who looked forlorn and confused, not understanding the lack of attention from the dark-haired woman.

Connie embraced and kissed her father, then plunged into Layne's arms. He held her tight, kissed her soundly, and released her. Leading her to the coach, he opened the door, helped her in, and closed it. Layne stepped back and gazed at Connie, framed in the window. The shadows across her emerald-green eyes gripped his heart.

Ozzie snapped the reins with a "Hee-yah!" and the bright red Concord rolled away.

Connie leaned from the window, looking back. Hastily wiping tears, she watched the man she loved standing tall and erect, etching this picture of him in her memory.

Layne stood firm until the stagecoach passed through the gate and disappeared. Then he turned and looked at the colonel.

"That's some woman we've got there, son," smiled Morgan Lee.

"Yes, sir." Layne sighed. "That's some woman."

Layne was returned to his cell. Feeling lonely and empty, he stood at his window, watching casual activity on the parade ground. Connie's words echoed through his mind: *Our lives will not really begin until the day you are free and we are together!* The coming of that day seemed like an eternity to Layne, but it would be the only thing he would have to hold on to while he sat in his prison cell, surrounded by the same walls, for the next five years.

The Concord had been gone nearly half an hour when Layne noticed the dispatcher emerge from the telegraph room and run hard for the colonel's house. Thinking nothing of it, Layne lay down on his cot and tried to take a nap.

Two minutes later young Corporal Stram darted from the house toward the prison building. Breathlessly, Stram said something to the guard on duty. Instantly the guard was inside, unlocking Layne's cell door. "Colonel Lee wants you, Britton. On the double."

The corporal ran alongside Layne as they made for the big white house. "What's this about?" asked Layne.

"I'd better let Colonel Lee tell you," gasped Stram.

Colonel Morgan Lee was standing behind his desk, a broad grin on his face, as Layne entered the office. A sheet of paper dangled from his fingers.

"Layne," asked Morgan, "do you know a teenage boy by the name of Danny Smith?"

"Yes, sir. He's the sweep boy at the Sunflower Hotel in Wichita."

"Apparently he has had a fondness for hanging around shady characters."

"That's right. I tried to talk sense into him. Told him he ought to stay away from them."

"Must have sunk in," said the silver-haired man, still smiling. "Because of him, you are a free man!"

Layne Britton's body went numb all over. "What?"

Shaking the paper in his hand, Morgan said, "This is a rather lengthy message from Marshal Roy Templeton. I'll explain it in brief. This Danny Smith was hired by Dolph Catron through one of his henchmen to sneak out to the Kellogg ranch and take those horses you and Connie had put in the corral."

Layne Britton's face began to crack into a smile.

Continuing, the colonel said, "This Smith kid got to thinking of what a terrible thing he had done in helping to frame you. He confessed it to Templeton this morning. Says he had no idea they were gonna bushwhack Boone Foss. When the marshal arrested this man Jack McQuaid who had hired the kid, McQuaid broke down and admitted it."

Lifting the paper, Morgan focused on it and said, "McQuaid named a W. D. Hunt as the man who borrowed your clothes while he shot Boone Foss. When Foss found this out, he got off his sickbed and went after Hunt. Well, Foss wasn't in the best of shape. . . . Hunt killed him this time."

Layne's heart was racing as the colonel said, "McQuaid and Hunt refused to bear sole responsibility for setting you up. They produced evidence on Dolph Catron. All three have been arrested and are in jail. Templeton says the county prosecutor is going to do his best to get Catron twenty years. Says it's as good as done already."

Shaking his head, Layne said, "It's a bit ironic."

"What's that?"

"After all Dolph Catron has done to you, you're probably the last man in the world he wants to see. Now he's going to be right under your nose, maybe till he dies!"

"Life is like that," grinned Morgan. "The Good Book says a man reaps what he sows."

Layne nodded silently.

Looking back at the paper, the colonel continued, "Templeton says to tell you that an attorney named Justin Barry has legally obtained the papers on the Kellogg ranch from Catron's files. You are to see Barry as soon as you get back. He adds that the whole town wants to make you an apology. They're going to do it up big at a spectacular barn dance in your honor. You and Connie are to be king and queen of the evening."

"Sounds great!" said Layne, choking on a lump in his throat. "How soon will I be released?"

"As fast as you can get out of that prison outfit and into your own."

Less than ten minutes had passed when Layne Britton emerged into the sunlight wearing his own clothes. Morgan Lee stood in the middle of the parade ground, holding the reins of a saddled horse with "U.S." branded on its rump. A uniformed man with three chevrons on his sleeve sat astride another horse of like brand.

As Layne approached, the colonel said, "These are two of our fastest horses. They'll catch up to the stagecoach in no time. Sergeant Lake here is going along so he can bring your horse back."

Layne smiled at the commandant. "Thank you, sir," he said with sincerity.

"You can thank me in two ways, *son*," grinned Morgan, emphasizing the last word.

"How's that?"

"Be sure I get an invitation to the wedding, and name your first boy *Morgan Lee Britton*."

"Consider it done, Dad," replied Layne, a grin lighting his whole face.

The blazing sun was turning the western sky into a farrago of red, orange, and purple when Layne Britton and Sergeant Lake spotted the tawny cloud of dust up ahead.

Pressing the lathered horses onward, they soon drew alongside the rocking, swaying stagecoach.

"Hey, Ozzie!" shouted Layne. "Pull up!"

The driver and shotgunner looked at each other in total shock.

The occupants of the stage peered out the windows into the dim light as the vehicle began to slow down. From her window, Connie had caught sight of Sergeant Lake's horse and blue uniform. Layne rode on the outside of Lake and was blocked from her view.

As the Concord rolled to a halt, Connie pushed her face into the window frame as one of the riders dismounted. Puddles was barking from the box, and Ozzie was saying something Connie could not distinguish. As her emerald eyes searched the area, she noticed a tall figure walking toward her.

"Layne!" she cried, opening the door. "How—?" For an instant she looked past him and was relieved to see that the sergeant was smiling.

Reaching into the coach, Layne took Connie's slender waist in both hands. He lifted her out and hugged her tightly. Holding her there with her feet barely touching the ground and wonderment in her eyes, he said, "How would you like to begin our lives right now?"

Coming in December 1984 . . .

From the creators of WAGONS WEST

STAGECOACH STATION 16:

MOJAVE

Out of the bleak, forbidding Mojave, some men dared to stake their claim to mining fortunes. Others like the wild-eyed Mexican bandit used the desert as a base for a bloody reign of terror through two countries. Grant Whitman took on the assignment of challenging the Mojave's unyielding, cruel dangers to hunt down Arango and his riders of death. To succeed he would need a tough hide, unwavering courage and the aid of an unexpected ally, Eustacia Kibbe, a defiant wife and mother caught up in her own search—for her husband, the very man who may hold the key to the life or death of Arango. And even as his trail leads closer to his deadly target, searing through Grant's brain is the burning truth that in this merciless Mojave, the odds would always favor the outlaw and the desert.

Don't miss STAGECOACH STATION 16: MOJAVE, available December 15, 1984, wherever Bantam Books are sold.

★ WAGONS WEST ★

A series of unforgettable books that trace the lives of a dauntless band of pioneering men, women, and children as they brave the hazards of an untamed land in their trek across America. This legendary caravan of people forge a new link in the wilderness. They are Americans from the North and the South, alongside immigrants, Blacks, and Indians, who wage fierce daily battles for survival on this uncompromising journey—each to their private destinies as they fulfill their greatest dreams.

☐	24408	**INDEPENDENCE!**	**$3.95**
☐	24651	**NEBRASKA!**	**$3.95**
☐	24229	**WYOMING!**	**$3.95**
☐	24088	**OREGON!**	**$3.95**
☐	24848	**TEXAS!**	**$3.95**
☐	24655	**CALIFORNIA!**	**$3.95**
☐	24694	**COLORADO!**	**$3.95**
☐	20174	**NEVADA!**	**$3.50**
☐	20919	**WASHINGTON!**	**$3.50**
☐	22925	**MONTANA!**	**$3.95**
☐	23572	**DAKOTA!**	**$3.95**
☐	23921	**UTAH!**	**$3.95**
☐	24256	**IDAHO!**	**$3.95**

Prices and availability subject to change without notice.

Buy them at your local bookstore or use this handy coupon: